T0389895

NIRA

A CONSTANCE EVERMORE STORY

THOMAS E. SNIEGOSKI & JEANNINE S. ACHESON

Bad Hand Books
www.badhandbooks.com

TOM:
*For Jeannine Acheson and Doug Murano for helping me
get the spark back.*

JEANNINE:
For Avis.

Nira

A Constance Evermore Story

Harry Derval never thought it would pass so quickly, but here it was, yet another day about to begin like so many that had come—and gone—before it.

"Same place as usual, Dad?" Ian asked, already knowing the answer, pushing Harry's wheelchair across the slightly warped hardwood floor of the barroom.

Harry grunted something that sounded like yes as his son wheeled him over to the open space between the end of the bar and the plate glass window that looked out onto the main drag that ran past Derval's Pub.

Locking the wheels in place, Ian left him there, going about his business of opening the bar for the day. From this spot, Harry could watch Derval's entrance, as well as the comings and goings of the townsfolk of Clark, Massachusetts, outside. This had been his spot from the earliest of days, when first opening the bar after he'd returned from overseas in '46 at the end of World War II, to now, even after being debilitated by multiple strokes.

It was his window to the world, however small it became with each passing day.

"You good?" Ian asked.

Harry looked away from the view to his son standing behind the bar. He nodded, even though he wasn't good at all. He hadn't been good for quite some time, since the first of his strokes in 1972, but that was neither here nor there.

"Okay, I'm headin' downstairs to finish up with the inventory, holler if you need me."

Harry had tried to keep up with the day to day operations of running the bar, but it got to be too much, especially as his health continued to worsen. Ian was a godsend, if it hadn't been for him moving back home Derval's would have been forced to shut its doors years ago and he would've ended up at the Acres, a real shithole and the only nursing home in the area.

Yeah, Ian returning to Clark saved far more than just the bar.

His son owed him nothing, their contact having been minimal after his leaving for college—they really never saw things eye to eye—but the death of Ian's mother, Harry's long-suffering wife, brought the boy

back to Massachusetts. It wasn't too long after that his son took pity on the wreck his father had become, offering to stay around for a while to help with the business, but when Harry suffered another in a series of debilitating strokes, Ian ultimately ended up not only taking on the bar, but his care as well.

The kid deserved better.

Wasn't that the thing parents always wished for their children? For them to have better—to have more than what their parents had before them? What did Ian have? A rundown saloon barely making enough to cover the bills, and an old man who needed help taking a piss, among other things. This isn't what he wanted for his son...

Or himself for that matter.

As a child of the Depression, Harry had always strived for more, never afraid to get his hands dirty, taking on as much work as he could find in order to help his parents support his younger brother and sisters. His contributions to the family continued even after his enlistment in the Army after the bombing of Pearl Harbor, the money he earned as a soldier being wired back home. Stationed in Europe he'd seen a great deal of action and more than once he thought for sure his life was over. Surviving the hell of war became his only objective, no thoughts of the future other than returning home in one piece.

Your story isn't finished, Harry.

He heard the words as if whispered in his ear, and jumped in his chair, heartbeat quickening with the memory of when he'd first heard them. With great effort, Harry turned his body to see behind the bar, eyes going to the place where a specific bottle of whiskey brought home with him from the war had been kept, put in a place of honor on the day he had first opened Derval's doors.

Nobody was ever to touch the bottle, and to this day it remained unopened.

He and the whiskey had been through a lot. A trophy to the fact that he'd survived a particular moment—that he'd survived the ordeal of war.

But *she* had said that he would.

Harry closed his eyes and remembered. It had been quite some time since he'd last thought of that night, how scared he'd been, and how sure he was that he was going to die.

In the midst of a harsh German winter, he'd become separated from his regiment in the Hürtgen Forest, Howitzer fire relentlessly raining down causing them to flee for their lives into the deep, dark wood. It had been so cold, the air thick with ice. Harry remembered how his lungs had burned as he'd run through the accumulating snow, his every sense on high alert waiting for German soldiers to emerge from hiding and shoot him down in a hail of gunfire. The sound of warfare echoed through the forest as he'd searched for the members of his regiment, but they were nowhere to be found. He was alone, cold and wet, and as night fell and the storm intensified he knew that if the enemy did not kill him, the harshness of the winter conditions certainly would.

Sitting in his wheelchair, Harry could still feel the brutality of the German cold as he'd felt it then, numbing his hands and feet. He'd never liked the winter much to begin with, but having survived Hürtgen Forest, he had learned to both hate and fear it.

Close to giving up, to lying down in the snow and drifting peacefully off to sleep, he glimpsed it through the swirling curtain of white. At first he had no idea what it was he was seeing, believing it was some sort of hallucination, a mirage taking form from the swirling curtain of white, but then realized that in fact there was something there. Finding a deep hidden reserve of strength within, Harry pushed through the heavy drifts, toward the looming shape that appeared to be just beyond the storm.

It was a house, a lovely Victorian, and Harry had never seen anything quite so beautiful.

He remembered, at that moment, being so

overjoyed that he didn't even question what a Victorian home would be doing in the middle of a German forest.

It didn't matter then, all he knew was this was a chance for him to live. The drifts fought to halt his progress, but Harry pushed on through the mounting accumulation. The closer he got, the farther the house seemed to be but it did not deter him until finally reaching the front steps that led up to a dark, wooden door. He remembered how strange it seemed to him that the six stairs were barren of snow, not a drop of the white stuff on any of their surfaces. Almost as if the home had somehow just arrived, and the freezing precipitation hadn't yet had the chance to accumulate.

There had been a moment's trepidation, but then the wind howled and the icy claws of the storm attempted to drag him back and claim him as its own, and Harry surged forward to climb the bare wooden steps.

Standing at the door he felt a sudden sense of calm, and slid the strap of his rifle over his shoulder, reaching for the ornate doorknob. There was a heat to the knob, he could feel it even through his soaked, wool gloves. He was sure that it would be locked, and had already begun to think of other ways he might enter the house when—

Klick!

The knob turned, and he pushed the door open into a comforting warmth that said to him, *come in, come in out of the cold.*

And Harry did as he was told.

He remembered how his voice had sounded in the air of the foyer as he called out.

"Hello? Is there anybody home? My name is Corporal Harry Derval and I'm with the 4th Infantry Division of the United States Army."

His pronouncements were met with an eerie silence as he carefully continued down a short hallway toward the kitchen. There was a metal-topped baking table in the room's center, a basket of strangely colored fruit that he could not identify sat upon one of the countertops and his stomach growled as he was tempted to sample one. A refrigerator hummed softly to itself in the corner, a multiple burnered cast iron stove was directly across from him. A tea kettle sat upon one of the burners, ready and waiting. The kitchen space was spotless, showing no obvious signs of use. Harry was about to call out again before moving on with his search for life when heard it, softly flowing into the silence.

Music.

He couldn't quite make out the tune, but turned around in the kitchen to head back in the direction he'd come—

But the doorway was no longer there.

Somehow a counter, with many cabinets above it, had replaced the way he'd entered.

Harry recalled the disconcerted feeling he'd experienced as he reached out to touch first the counter, and then the cabinets above it. They had been solid to the touch, but how…

Focusing on the music, his eyes fell upon a swinging door in the far corner of the room. Harry walked quickly to the door, fearful that something might happen to this exit as well, and he'd be trapped.

The door opened into a large pantry, its many shelves filled with canisters and glass jars. He was momentarily curious as to what might be stored in such a large amount of containers, but the music drew him through another swinging door that took him out of the pantry into a dining room. A long rectangular table of walnut sat in the center, a beautiful crystal chandelier hanging above it. Harry noticed a setting for one had been placed at the far end of the stately piece of furniture.

The music was louder, drifting in from beyond the rounded doorway and he followed it out of the dining room down another hallway, the walls on either side decorated with framed pieces of art, as well as photographs in all sizes and shapes. Harry looked at the pictures as he passed, people of varying ages and sex, but all the photographs had one thing in particular in common: behind the subjects of the photos, there sat a house, an old Victorian.

This house.

But its location in each of the photographs was different. There were mountains in the background of some, ocean vistas in others, crowded city neighborhoods with homes on either side, but there was no doubt that it was the same house.

The lilting tune he'd been following came to a sudden end. Harry stood, listening—waiting, as another song, this time something more recognizable, began.

There was a comfort in the music, something that put him more at ease as he searched the strange house for signs of life. Leaving the paintings and photographs behind, he walked to the end of the hallway where a large set of double doors awaited him. Leaning in close, he could hear that the music was coming from the other side.

He raised a hand, about to knock when—

"Hello, Harry."

The man's eyes had been closed as he remembered back to a day which, as the years marched on, seemed more and more like an unreality, a strange manifestation of his imagination.

The voice that stirred him from his reverie was from a time before…

But this was now.

She had come into the bar as silently as a memory.

For the briefest of moments he thought himself hallucinating, the images inside his mind from the past leaking into the present day.

He recalled her voice from behind the double doors calling out for him to come in before he'd had a chance to knock.

Hesitantly, he turned the knob and pushed open one of the doors. A single lamp lit the room—a study— the walls lined with bookshelves, an old Victrola like the one his grandmother had, played the recording of a classical piece filling the space with music. Beneath the light source a woman sat, long legs crossed. Her hair was shockingly white, her gaunt face pale. She did not look at him as she flipped through a copy of *Life* magazine.

"Are you here to do me harm?" she asked casually, flipping the pages, her dark eyes going from one page to the next.

"No, I..."

"Good," she said, looking briefly away from her reading to glance to a deeply shadowed area in the far corner of the room before returning her attention to the magazine.

"I don't care for that."

The bodies of two German soldiers lay unmoving within the deep patch of shadow. For no reason he could articulate, he knew that they were dead.

"My name is Corporal Harry—"

"Derval of the 4th Infantry Division," the woman finished as she turned another page. "I heard you earlier."

She looked up at him. "My name is Constance Evermore. Why are you in my house?"

"Hello," Harry said sheepishly. "There... there was a battle in the forest... I was separated from my battalion... searching for a place to... I found your house."

"That's what those two said," Constance said, hooking a thumb over her shoulder. "Only in German, right before they announced they were commandeering my home for the glory of the Third Reich. Like hell, they were."

She'd reached the end of the magazine and stuffed it into the side of the chair.

The record on the Victrola had come to an end,

and silence filled the room. Far off in the distance outside there were sounds like thunder.

"You thought you were going to die," Constance said, moving the foot of her crossed leg up and down.

"Yeah," he said, remembering the intensity of his fear. "I was pretty sure it was over for me."

"It's not over for you," the mysterious woman said, looking deeply into his eyes and slowly shaking her head. "Your story isn't finished, Harry."

And it wasn't, there were still many experiences still to be lived, years to be knocked back as he remembered the woman's—Constance's—words, all the while wondering when he would finally reach the end.

"Nice to see you again, Harry."

She strode further into the bar, hands stuffed deep into the pockets of her flowing coat, looking exactly as she had some forty years ago when he'd seen her last, when she had welcomed him into her home, providing him with a safe place from the storm—from the war.

He wanted to go to her, to enwrap this strange part of his history in his arms once more, holding on for all it was worth, but not all of the pages of his story had been kind. Especially the later ones.

"Let me have a look at you," she said, leaning in close.

He closed his eyes and breathed her in. She smelled of fall, of turning leaves, of smokey autumn days with a hint of spice. Cloves, he believed.

Looking up into her face, he saw that she was exactly the same as she had been the last time he had seen her. The deep dark eyes, their color indeterminable even this close, hair snow white, skin like alabaster.

He remembered her kindness, allowing him to sleep on a red velvet couch in the house's parlor, but at sunrise she told him that it was time to leave.

She told him he had to get on with his story, and she with her own.

"You look like hell," Constance said, looking him over. "But you're still here, I was right about that."

She'd been so certain that he would survive the war, that she had given him a gift.

"Do you still have it?" she asked, looming over him.

His eyes answered for him.

Constance had opened the door, a blast of cold air and snow rushing in to swirl about them where they stood. There was a stillness to the morning, the sounds of warfare not yet awakened.

"Thank you," Harry had said, shifting his rifle from one shoulder to the other, tentatively holding out his hand to her. "I'm not sure I would've made it if I hadn't…"

"Probably not," she said. "But you did."

From behind her back she produced something wrapped in beige muslin and handed it to him.

"What's this?" he'd asked, taking her offering.

"Something to celebrate the journey."

He partially unwrapped the cloth to see that she'd given him a bottle of whiskey.

"Hey now," Harry said with a chuckle. "This is somethin'."

"It's a favorite of mine, old like me," Constance said, a certain weight to her words hinting at a much deeper meaning.

"I can't take this, I should be giving you something," Harry said, trying to hand the bottle back.

"It's yours, Harry," Constance told him. "I think there's a reason you stumbled across my house. Get you, and the bottle home safely, and maybe we'll have the chance to share a drink some day."

"Wouldn't that be somethin'," Harry said, taking back the bottle.

"Wouldn't it?" the woman said as she watched him wrap the bottle again, and slide it carefully inside his jacket for safe keeping.

"The house is getting cold," Constance said.

"Right. I better get goin' so you can close the door."

"Be well, Harry," she said as he stepped onto the porch. "Until next time."

He recalled the finality of the click of the door behind him as he walked across the porch of the old Victorian. Part of him wanted to turn and pound upon the door begging to be let back in, but he knew he couldn't do that. He had hesitated, just before descending the steps to the feet of snow that had continued to fall during the night. As he waded through the icy drifts that awaited him, the woods came alive with the sounds of movement, something emerging through the trees toward him. He wondered if this was the moment when it would all end, but the strange warmth of the bottle nestled safely inside his jacket assured him somehow that it was not.

"**B**ehind the bar?" Constance asked him.

Harry slowly nodded.

"Don't get up, let me," she said, moving around his chair to get behind the bar.

With effort he turned the wheelchair so he could watch her.

"Bet you thought you'd never see me again," Constance said, perusing the shelves of liquor, looking for the bottle she had given him those many years ago.

She was right. There had been many instances when

he thought that maybe the memory of her had all been some bizarre figment of his imagination, a hallucination brought on by the lingering stress of battle.

He was taking the rifle from his shoulder to defend himself against a possible attack when members of his unit emerged from the forest.

"Hey, Derval, that you?"

He recognized the voice right off, Private 2nd Class James Palmiotti from Brooklyn. Other members of his division trudged through the snow behind him.

"Ain't you a sight for sore eyes," Harry had said.

"A face only a mother could love," Palmiotti answered. "Where the heck you been, we thought you was a goner!"

"You and me both," he said. "Got lost in the storm, but then I found this house and…"

He remembered the feeling in the pit of his stomach as he had turned to point out the Victorian to his fellow soldier when he came to the disturbing realization that the house was gone.

"Did you say you found a house?" Palmiotti asked, sidling up alongside him, looking to where Harry stared in disbelief.

He was going to explain, to tell the Private about

the mysterious place that he'd stumbled across in the snow, and the strange woman that lived there, but…

"Naw, no house," Harry said. "I was hiding out in the woods hoping I'd find you guys before Uncle Adolf's boys found me."

As he spoke he continued to look at the spot where the Victorian had been, the ground only now starting to be covered by the falling snow. At that moment he had started to question if any of it had happened at all, when he felt the weight of the bottle against his chest inside his jacket and the uncertainty drifted away—like an old house in a German forest.

"Where the hell did you put it?" She stepped back some, trying to take it all in, eyes moving across the shelves as she searched.

Harry grunted, and she looked his way as he slowly raised a flaccid hand to point.

He'd managed to keep the whiskey safe and unsampled until his time in the service to his country was over and he had made the long journey back home to civilian life. There had been times when his resolve had been tested, tempting him to crack the seal and indulge in the golden liquid contained in the gift bottle from a mysterious, white haired woman.

Though whenever the urge struck, something told him that it wasn't yet time and the desire was quelled. The unopened bottle became a sort of trophy of his survival, an award signifying that he not only managed to live through the worst that humanity could throw at him, but also that he managed not to crumble under the weight of the psychic scar tissue that he bore upon his return from Europe. Despite all he had endured, he had continued on with his life, starting a business and having a family.

The bottle was a symbol of his triumph over adversity, and an item such as that deserved a place of honor.

Her gaze followed to where he pointed.

"Look at that, hiding in plain sight," Constance said, reaching to take the whiskey from its special place in the center of the shelf, slightly elevated, yet surrounded by other bottles of varying heights. "And still sealed, I'm proud of you, Harry."

Constance admired the Merriman's 12-year-old single malt.

"Hello, old friend," she said fondly, lovingly caressing the bottle with her thumb.

She looked over at him and smiled slyly. "So, what do you say, Harry? Should we finally have that drink?"

He was about to answer, when—

"Hey! Excuse me, what the hell do you think you're doing?" Ian demanded, coming up from the cellar.

"We're about to have a drink," Constance said. "Let me guess, you're the spawn of Harry."

"Who the hell are you?"

"An old friend," she said, looking over to him. "Isn't that right, Harry?"

He nodded vigorously, trying to explain to his son, but the words wouldn't come, it was so hard since the strokes.

"You're not supposed to be behind the bar," Ian said. He stormed over, grabbing the whiskey out of Constance's hand. "And you shouldn't be touching this!"

Ian returned the bottle to its place of honor where it had sat for decades. "We don't officially open up 'till noontime so I think you should…"

"No," Harry managed, slamming his hands down upon the armrests of his wheelchair.

"Dad?" Ian asked, surprised by his father's response.

"No, Ian," he said again. "Wa…wait… waiting." Harry struggled to get the words out. "Waiting… for… her."

Ian looked to the woman.

"Who the hell *are* you?"

"I've had many names," she said, a weariness to her answer. "But your father met me as Constance Evermore."

"You gave him the bottle," Ian said. "During the war."

"I did," Constance said.

"But that was forty years ago, and you don't look…"

"It was, and thank you."

"This is fucking crazy," Ian said, looking to his father. "Dad?"

"It… her," Harry struggled to get the words out.

"It's me, Ian," Constance said. "Could I have that bottle back?"

"I don't understand any of this," Ian said, taking the bottle from where he'd just placed it and tentatively handing it back to the woman.

"And I'm really not sure that you're meant to," she said, taking it from him. "I'd suspected that your father and I would cross paths again, that there was a reason he'd ended up at my house."

"We always thought he was makin' stuff up," Ian said, looking at his father. "War stories and shit."

Harry closed his eyes, vindicated after all these years.

"No idea how we would connect again, or when, but if there's anything I have plenty of, it's time…" She pulled the cork from the bottle with a satisfying pop. "And patience."

Constance closed her eyes as she sniffed the opening.

"Ahhh, that's the stuff," she said. "Get us some glasses, would you?"

Ian hesitated, but did as he was told. "So you just stumbled across the bar and…"

"There's no stumbling," she said. "I needed to be here so I came. Your father—and this whiskey—is just a nice surprise and the answer to a question we've both carried for a very long time. Isn't that right, Harry?"

Harry smiled, still in awe of the woman standing there.

Ian came back with two tumblers.

"Three," Constance said.

"Dad can't have any, as you can probably see he's not in the best of shape."

"Three," she repeated more firmly.

"But…"

"No buts."

"Three," Harry repeated with some difficulty.

Ian rolled his eyes getting another glass. "I'm not going to be responsible if it kills him."

"That's the spirit," Constance said as Ian placed the tumblers and she began to pour at least two fingers worth into each. She put the cork back in the bottle and set it down.

She picked up one of the glasses and handed it to Ian. "Here you go," she said, taking another of the tumblers and turning toward Harry.

"He's probably gonna need some help with that," Ian said. "The strokes have taken away his ability to…"

"He'll be fine," Constance said, carefully placing the drink in Harry's hand and holding it in both of hers.

"You got this?" she asked him, her dark eyes locking onto his, and he knew that he did.

"Yes."

"Okay then," Constance said, picking up the last of the three tumblers. "A toast, then."

They waited to hear what she would say as she seemed to be thinking.

"To crossed paths," Constance said, raising her glass. "There's always a reason."

She tossed back the golden liquid without pause, Ian following suit.

With great effort Harry lifted the glass to his eager mouth, anticipating what he had waited so very long to sample. The whiskey flowed into his mouth, over his tongue and down his throat. The burn exquisite, and a warmth flowed through his body, as he was reminded of one of the simplest of life's pleasures taken from him since his health had turned.

"Worth the wait?" Constance asked him.

Harry just smiled.

"So, if you're not here to see my father, what are

you doing here?" Ian asked, setting his empty tumbler down upon the bar.

"Business," Constance answered, uncorking the bottle and pouring herself some more of the single malt. "Business of a potentially malevolent nature." She drank the whiskey down. "There is somebody who is going to be looking for me... somebody who needs my help."

"And they'll be coming to this bar?" Ian asked.

"Looks to be the perfect place for a meeting, quiet, cozy, I know the staff and they serve my whiskey."

She grabbed the bottle of Merriman's single malt and her glass, and came out from behind the bar.

"So what will you do till then?" Ian asked.

She considered the question for a moment.

"I'm going to find myself a table as far back in the shadows as I can, drink some more whiskey, and I'm going to wait. It shouldn't be long. It never is."

Constance looked at Harry as she passed, and he experienced another glorious flush of warmth.

"I told you your story wasn't finished and look at all you have done," she said, walking away from him. "You done good, Harry."

He had never really thought to be proud of his life, at what he had accomplished. He hadn't discovered the cure for cancer, or won the Nobel Peace Prize, but he did come home from war, battered and scarred, raised a family, and started a business. Sure, he wished his health had been better but there wasn't anything definitive that said his life would have been much different even if it had.

Harry had done as he was supposed to do.

He lived.

Constance walked to the back of the bar, staring down all the tables before making her choice.

This is the one, she thought, pulling out a chair and sitting down. Situating herself, she placed the whiskey bottle to her left, empty glass in front of her ready to be refilled. She paused for a moment before reaching deep inside her coat to remove a leather pouch, placing it down carefully upon the table.

Pleased that all was in order, the woman who now went by the name Constance Evermore, poured herself another whiskey.

And waited.

Frances Stafford had passed by the window of Derval's Pub on more than a few occasions, when she'd come to town to shop, but not being much of a drinker, had never gone inside.

Stopping at the entrance, she again checked the

worn business card to be certain she was in the right place.

"Is this it, Mama?" the little girl holding her mother's hand asked, looking up at the gold lettered sign over the entrance.

"I think it is," Frances said, though, strangely enough she remembered a time when the card had no address at all. When her husband had first found the card sticking to the glass of their wet storm door after a particularly violent summer squall, it had simply read, *I can help*, in cursive with the name, *C. Evermore: Inquisitor of the Uncanny* beneath the missive. No phone number, no address...

At first.

When things started to get bad at the house, she'd stumbled across the card again, and suddenly, where there had been none before, there was an address.

"Are we gonna go in?" her daughter asked.

This was the address.

"Yes," she said, reaching for the door handle. "We have to."

Frances pulled open the door into the cool, dimly lit entryway. It took a moment for her eyes to adjust to the subdued lighting.

"It smells funny in here," Livy said, wrinkling her nose.

The child was right, the barroom having the distinct smell of multiple alcohols spilled over the decades.

"Hush," Frances said, pulling the child further into the drinking establishment. She immediately felt eyes upon her, men at tables looking up from their drinks, others turning to stare from barstools.

She caught the eyes of an old man sitting in a wheelchair alongside the bar, and he slowly raised a shaking hand, motioning her closer.

Holding her daughter's hand tightly, Frances approached a younger man tending bar, who had just finished serving a customer when he noticed her.

"Can I help you, hon?" he asked, clearing away some empty beer bottles, storing them somewhere below the bartop. Frances hesitated, eyes darting around the bar.

"I gotta say," the bartender said. "You look a bit out of your element."

She was about to speak up when—

"We're lookin' for the person who's supposed to help us," Livy told the man.

By the expression that crossed his face it seemed as though the man knew what her daughter was talking about.

"We're looking for this person," Frances said, handing the man the mysterious business card.

He took the card, read it and quickly handed it back as he started to come around the bar.

"I think it's them," he said to the man in the wheelchair as he passed. The old man nodded, gesturing for the younger man to go on.

"Come with me," the bartender said as he walked past them on his way across the floor.

Frances and Livy followed the man as he spoke casually to customers, sharing a laugh or a friendly pat on the shoulder on his way toward the back of the establishment. He paused briefly to make sure they still followed. They were going so far back that Frances began to think that he was bringing them to a backdoor to show them out.

Abruptly the man turned and headed toward a table in the corner at the farthest end of the bar. Frances saw that an older woman was sitting there, a bottle of liquor to the side of her, a glass held in her hand. There was a pouch, or maybe it was her purse, sitting in the center of the table. Her eyes were closed, and Frances thought that maybe she was asleep.

The bartender cleared his throat, and the woman's eyes slowly opened. Frances noticed how dark her eyes were, and thought it had to be a curious trick of the light—or lack thereof—at the back of the room.

"You said you were waiting for somebody," the man said to the older woman.

"Yes."

"I think this is them," he said, motioning with his thumb to where they stood.

"Thank you," she said. "You can go."

The bartender turned and quickly walked by them.

"Good luck," he muttered beneath his breath on his way back up to the front.

"Thank you," Frances told him, before returning her attention to the white haired woman sitting at the table.

"Are you looking for me?" the woman asked.

Frances fumbled for the card and presented it.

"Is this you?" she asked hopefully.

She studied the card and nodded slowly. "Yes, I'm Constance Evermore."

"Then we are looking for you."

The old woman studied them both with unblinking eyes. Again, Frances found herself fascinated by their shiny blackness.

"Okay then," the white haired woman said, picking up the bottle and removing the cork. She poured herself a very large drink.

"Why don't you two take a seat and tell me how I can help."

Frances pulled out her chair, and reached over to do the same for her daughter.

"I can do it," Livy said confidently, pulling the seat out on her own and climbing onto the chair, knees first.

Frances sat as well.

The older woman lifted the glass to her mouth, stopping midway.

"Can I get you some whiskey, Miss… "

"Mrs. Mrs. Paul Stafford. I'm Frances. No, thank you," she answered. "I'm fine."

Constance turned her attention to Livy. "You?"

"I'm six," she answered.

"Beer, then?"

"Livy is good, Ms. Evermore," Frances said, her curiosity about this woman continuing to escalate.

"Suit yourself," she said, completing the whiskey's journey to her mouth and downing the contents.

"You must be very thirsty," Livy said as the woman sat her empty glass down.

"You need to be quiet now," Frances said, reaching over to briefly squeeze the back of her daughter's arm.

"She's right, I am thirsty," Constance said, grabbing the bottle again and filling her glass halfway.

An uneasy silence fell over the table, and Frances was on the verge of vocalizing that this might have been mistake when—

"But, enough about me," Constance said, a sad smile unfurling upon her pale face. "What can I do for *you*?"

Frances had no idea where to start, placing the tattered business card down upon the table's sticky surface.

"We found this," she said, "and seeing as things… things have become difficult, I thought—*we thought*—that maybe… what harm could there be if…"

"There are ghosts in our house," Livy interjected impatiently.

"Livy!"

"Ghosts?" Constance said, carefully sipping from her glass. "Tell me more."

"I know it must sound ridiculous," Frances began. "But…"

"No," the old woman interrupted. "You tell me." She pointed a long finger at Livy.

Livy glanced over, seeking permission to speak.

"Go ahead," Frances told her.

"We moved to a new house when I was little and Mommy and Daddy were fixing it up and we found out ghosts lived there!"

"You don't say," Constance said, seemingly with genuine interest.

"Yes," Livy said. "And they are very noisy and made my daddy sick."

"Sick?"

Constance looked to Frances for further clarification.

"My husband has recently taken ill, yes," Frances said.

"And you think the ghosts are responsible?"

"I really don't know what to think," Frances answered, feeling her resolve begin to crumble. "Nobody seems to know what's wrong with him. One moment he was fine, and the next…"

"He doesn't get out of bed," Livy added. "He's very tired all the time."

"Tell me about this house," Constance said.

"Nothing much to tell really," Frances said. "It's an old farm house in Bethany Falls, built in the mid-1800s. We fell in love with the place the first time we set eyes on it. It was going to need a lot of work, but we were up for the challenge."

"Any history of malfeasance?" Constance asked.

"Well, it was a small, family-owned working farm until it was sold in 1925 to Vincent Tomesello, a New York gangster and bootlegger who owned the property up until sometime in the early 1930's. The place sat empty until my husband and I purchased it three years ago."

"Gangster and bootlegger," Constance said thoughtfully. "I bet the old place has some stories to tell."

"I'm sure it does," Frances agreed. "We pretty much began to notice the strange activity as soon as we moved in; footsteps all hours of the night, mysterious voices when there wasn't anybody else at home, objects being moved only to be found in the oddest of places."

"Weird sounds in the basement," Livy added, a tremble of fear in her young voice.

"Now my husband is sick, and I didn't know what to do—until I remembered the card." She drummed her fingers nervously on the business card. "You're our last hope, Constance Evermore," Frances said. "It says on the card that you can help.

Will you help us?"

A haunted farmhouse.
  Ghosts.

That's it? Constance wondered.

Not the all-encompassing evil requiring her services that was usually the norm.

Constance took the whiskey bottle, refreshed her glass with a large splash and proceeded to drink it down.

Ghosts. She knew all about them.

"Will you help us, Miss Evermore?" Frances asked again. "I'm not sure if we could pay you but—"

Constance raised a hand.

"I don't charge for my services," she said.

"Oh, that's wonderful," Frances said. "So you'll help?"

"I didn't say that," Constance answered.

She could feel the little girl's eyes upon her.

"I need to think about it," Constance explained. "There are things to consider before I make a decision."

"Things to consider?" Frances asked. "I don't understand. What kinds of things are we talking about?"

Constance shrugged. "Things."

"Is there anything that I could explain further? I assure you that I wouldn't have come here looking for you if—"

"I understand all that," Constance said. "I'm just going to need a little time, is all."

The child appeared disappointed, looking to her mother to say the thing that would convince her.

"We're desperate, Miss Evermore."

"It shouldn't take me long," Constance said, pouring another two fingers of whiskey into her glass and feeling especially thirsty at the moment.

"Then I guess we're done here," Frances said, pushing her chair back. "C'mon, Livy, if we move quickly we can catch the next bus home."

"You're not gonna help us?" Livy asked, climbing down from her chair.

"I said I need to think about it," Constance answered, turning the whiskey glass slowly, watching the golden liquid slosh around.

"The card said you can help," the child continued.

"It says I can, not that I will," Constance said.

"Let's go, Livy," Frances said, turning to leave the pub. "We'll leave Ms. Evermore to her thoughts and thirst."

Livy started to follow her mother, but stopped, turning around to return to the table.

"Forget something?" Constance asked the six year old standing before her.

"I really do hope you will help us," Livy said. "I don't want to be scared for my parents anymore."

Livy continued to stand there, waiting for something.

"You done?" Constance asked.

The little girl nodded, just as her mother called for her.

"Hurry up, we're going to miss the bus."

"Go on," Constance said. "Don't want to miss the bus."

She stood a moment longer, before turning and running to catch up with her mother.

"Bye," she said from over her shoulder, taking her mother's hand as the pair walked from the bar.

She was going to have more of the Merriman's but decided against it. Placing the cork back in the bottle, Constance left her table and returned to the bar. It took a moment for her to be noticed, but she motioned for Ian to come over, handing the bottle back to him.

"This can go back now," she told him.

"Don't you want to take it with you?" he asked. "Dad said it was yours."

"For next time," she said.

Ian glanced over to the left where his father still sat, now sound asleep in his wheelchair.

"Yeah," he said, a little sadder than the moment before. "Next time."

He turned away to carefully put the bottle back in its place of honor as she went to say goodbye to his father.

"Goodnight, Harry, great to see you again."

Harry twitched and moaned deep in the thralls of sleep. She knew that he was dreaming of the war, the cold, and a mysterious house waiting for him in the German forest.

Her house.

The house provided her with shelter and a place to rest so that she would remember the times from before, what had been lost, and what needed to be done to make amends for what she had failed to do.

They had been together for a very long time. It had not always been an elegant Victorian; through the ages, it had been a hut of grass and mud, a fieldstone hovel, a rustic log cabin, an abode made of stretched animal skins across tree limbs, and even, for a period, the deepest and darkest of caves.

Currently, it was a Queen Anne Victorian painted in soft tones of green and brown, and it waited for Constance where it had appeared hours ago between a run-down Dutch Colonial and a rickety old garage used for storage by one of the local machine shops. To see the Victorian suddenly there, in all its stately glory, one would not recall having ever seen it before, but there it was—

Until it wasn't.

For now, this was where the house would remain, a place for her to return to during the quiet moments when the burden of her purpose wasn't quite as heavy, but also a place where she would be reminded of an age before this one and how her arrogance had led to its total obliteration.

"Home," she called out as she passed through the open entryway into the house, the door closing softly behind her. She was thinking of today and the reacquaintance she had made, of the most excellent whiskey drunk, and the mother and daughter who had told her of their troubles.

It wasn't long before the ghost of her grandmother materialized in the hallway in front of her, long hair floating around her head in a halo of gray.

"How was your night?" Constance said, passing through the coldness of the old woman's body without a pause. "That's nice, I'm heading to the lounge, I need a drink."

The ghost trailed behind her as she entered the room. Constance dropped her bag onto an elaborately carved wooden coffee table, and shed her coat, draping it over the back of a wingback chair close by.

From the corner of her eye she watched as the old woman waited in the doorway.

Her grandmother appeared as she always did, her flowing raiments of yellow and gold indicating her status as tribal elder.

"I had some Merriman's tonight," Constance said, walking to the bar in the corner of the room. "It was really lovely, I'd forgotten how much I enjoyed it."

The ghost continued to hover in the entryway to

the lounge, bobbing in the ethereal winds like a buoy tossed by the sea.

"I wish I had some here, but if I remember correctly I drank most of it during the sixties." Hand poised over a wide variety of alcohols, she decided what might be an appropriate chaser for the fine whiskey she'd had earlier.

"Think I'll just go with brandy," she said, choosing a bottle, removing the cork with a deep pop, and giving it a sniff. "Yeah, this'll do for now."

Grabbing a snifter from the top of the bar she poured the amber colored liquid liberally, replaced the cork, and brought her drink to the overstuffed sofa across from the ornately carved coffee table.

The old woman watched her expectantly from the doorway with dark, bottomless eyes.

Constance lowered herself down onto her seat, careful not to spill her drink.

"Well, Nira-Ulah?" the ghost of her grandmother asked petulantly.

Constance knew that Nana Cyra was annoyed when she addressed her by her full original name.

"Well what, Nana?" Constance—*Nira-Ulah*—answered, putting her feet up onto the coffee table, sipping from her glass.

Nana Cyra flowed into the room in a rush of cold

air. "Well, what?" the ghost asked, her voice climbing in anger. "Well, what, you ask me? Have you grown stupid over the days?" Nana Cyra asked angrily.

"Hours," Constance corrected her. "I've only been gone hours. But it could have been years for all you know, ghosts really do have problems with the passage of time."

"And what have you come to know in these—hours?"

"I don't know," Constance said. "I haven't decided."

"There is darkness in the vicinity, yes? It is why the dwelling has brought you here."

"Yes, there's something here, and yes, it's probably dark, but I'm not sure that it requires my involvement."

"If there is evil, it requires you," Nana said. "This is why you are here—why you exist."

"I am completely aware of this, Nana, but thank you so much for the reminder," Constance said.

"Insolent pup," Nana growled.

"There is evil everywhere in this world, some far greater than others," she drank more of her brandy. "But others…"

"Some others are not worthy of your attention. Is that what you are saying, Nira-Ulah?" Nana Cyra asked her.

"No, I'm… ," Constance began, trying to explain. "I'm tired, Nana, and to have a moment when…"

"The evil, it is yours," the ghost of the old woman said. "It is your responsibility—no matter how small."

She downed the remainder of her drink and stood suddenly, heading back to the bar.

"You will do as you have always done," Nana Cyra ordered, the multiple bracelets upon her spectral wrist clattering aggressively, as she jammed a long, gnarled finger in the air.

"I will have another drink, and maybe another or two after that," Constance said, reaching the bar. She selected a dusty bottle of scotch from the bar. "And then I will decide, but not a moment sooner."

This infuriated the old ghost, and she began to angrily mutter beneath her breath in a language so old there wasn't anyone currently alive who knew that the civilization that spoke it had ever even existed.

"This is all because of you... this belongs to you!"

"Thank you for reminding me. Now, if you would be so kind as to leave me in peace, I'd like to enjoy my drink and come about with my decision."

Nana Cyra's angry voice went suddenly quiet, and Constance looked up to see that she was gone.

"Good," she said, finding a suitable glass and pouring the scotch whiskey. "One would think after the first few millennia she would finally understand that—"

"You really shouldn't be so hard on the old girl," a familiar voice said from someplace in the room.

"Wonderful," Constance said. "Another one to tell me my business."

The strange creature of black feathers and fur sauntered across the Oriental carpet from a shadow in the corner of the room toward her.

They looked as if a fox and crow had been somehow smashed together, a far more attractive looking beast than one would expect. This was Kaw, the last of their kind from a time before.

And often a gigantic pain in the ass.

"I'm doing no such thing, darling," the animal said. They sat down upon their haunches and admired one of their talons. "Though I am curious about your day. Might I ask what sort of evil you were alerted to? Was it great or, perhaps small? I'm curious."

Constance returned to the couch with her drink.

"Ghosts," Constance said, sitting down.

"Ghosts?" Kaw padded around the sofa, hopping up onto the cushion opposite her with a soft flutter of ebony wings. "What kind of ghosts?" the animal asked. "There's such a wide variety."

"Nothing special," Constance told them. "The haunting kind. Old farmhouse, used to belong to a mobster." She shrugged and drank some scotch. "Though it did make the little girl's father sick."

"Little girl?" Kaw asked with a slight tilt of its triangular shaped head.

"Yes," Constance said with a nod. "A mother and little girl."

"A mother and little girl in a haunted farmhouse where a ghost has made the mother's husband, and the little girl's father, sick? Is that it?"

"Pretty much."

"Well, that's not at all an earthshaking threat, is it?" the animal asked.

The scotch was good, as it always was, adding a fuzzy warmth to the buzz she already had.

"No, but I'm sure there's more."

"There's always more, isn't that always the way?"

"Yes," Constance agreed.

"And you did wind up in this place for a reason," Kaw added.

"Yeah, there was a guy who I'd met long ago holding a bottle of whiskey for me, but I don't think that's the reason the house brought me here."

"I doubt it," Kaw said. "When has the dwelling ever brought you anywhere for something nice?"

"This is true."

"Maybe the guy with the whiskey was the way to ease you into what's to follow?"

"Possibly."

"Then you can't really ignore this one," Kaw said. "The little girl, her mother and sick father in the haunted house."

"No," Constance said, tipping back her glass to capture the last of the whiskey. "You're probably right."

The temperature in the air of the lounge suddenly became freezing, as if the windows of an Arctic research station had been opened to air the place out. Constance glanced over from where she sat to see that she and Kaw had been joined by more ghostly presences, an entire room jammed full to be precise, their spectral numbers trailing out of the lounge, into the corridor and the rest of the house as well.

An angry looking Nana Cyra was positioned in the front of the gathering, having returned with backup.

"And I doubt they'd let me."

Livy Stafford awoke in the darkness of her bedroom with a start, heart fluttering in her chest so hard she thought it might explode. For a moment she lay there, not quite sure where she was, the faintest hint of a dream, of a beautiful jungle that had covered up the world, fleeing her thoughts as she opened her eyes.

Certain that something had taken her from

slumber, she searched the room, listening for any unfamiliar sound. The bedroom appeared okay, things familiar to her even shrouded in shadow, causing no concern. The farmhouse itself was quiet as well. As old as it was, there were always bumps and creaks, but tonight her house seemed to be—

From somewhere outside her room she heard the moan, and froze where she lay.

There had been moans before, and the sounds of heavy footsteps up and down the hallway in the night. The ghosts that lived here could be very noisy, but they didn't make this sound.

Livy knew who had made it, throwing back the covers and climbing from her bed. Crossing the room she opened her door and stepped out into the hallway—listening.

The moan was even louder out there.

Bare feet thumping across the hardwood floor, she ran the length of the hallway to a closed door at the end. Someone moaned pitifully on the other side, spurring her to open the door.

The smell of the room made her nose wrinkle, but she knew her daddy couldn't help it because he was sick.

"Daddy?" she spoke softly into the darkness.

A pitiful moan filled the air.

Moonlight shone in from the window, illuminating the bed in a silvery light. Her father lay upon his back, covered with only a sheet, his exposed skin made deathly pale in the glow of the moon.

Livy approached the bed.

"Daddy, you okay?" she asked, reaching out to place her hand upon her father's. The top of his hand was cold, clammy. The man twitched wildly, letting out a frightened yelp, causing her to pull away.

"Daddy?"

Livy watched her father focus in on her voice, his eyes blinking rapidly as the realization of who was there came over his pale face.

"Livy," he said tentatively, nodding with his head still upon the pillow, as if wanting to be sure.

"It's me, Daddy," she said, daring again to come closer to the bed. "I heard you moaning and wanted to make sure you were okay."

She didn't know if he had heard her and again reached out cautiously to touch his bony, bare shoulder sticking out from beneath the sheet. Livy noticed how skinny he had become, remembering the person he'd been when they'd first moved into the farmhouse. That man was big and strong and had a contagious laugh that could make her smile no matter how sad she was feeling.

That man was gone now, but she hoped that he might come back someday.

Maybe if Miss Evermore comes to help us, Livy thought hopefully.

Her father reacted as if he'd somehow heard her thinking.

"No… no one can help me," he strained, the words seeming to hurt as they came out. "I… I'm not… strong enough."

"You're fine, Daddy," Livy said, wanting with all her heart to believe. "You just need to rest… to get stronger."

"Was never strong enough," her father said, wincing in pain, the skin around his sunken eyes dark as if bruised. "He tells me that all the time… wanting me to just give up."

"Who tells you that, Daddy?" Livy asked.

Her father turned his head and stared deeply into her eyes, tears welling with his gaze.

"Livy," her father said.

"Yes, Daddy?"

"You're gonna die in this house and then you'll live here forever," a voice suddenly not her father's said, and then began to laugh, tossing his head back upon the sweat stained pillow. "Forever and ever and ever and ever…"

Livy backed slowly away from the bed as the man continued to laugh.

"You're not my daddy," she said, knowing this to be true.

The man stopped laughing and slowly sat up, his eyes glinting wetly in the rays of silver coming in through the window.

"Smart kid," the man said, lip raising in a snarl. "Yeah, he's in here with me, but not for much longer."

"You leave him alone!" Livy screamed, stamping her bare foot upon the hardwood floor. "Don't you dare hurt my daddy!"

The man who wasn't her father smiled a smile so wide she thought his face might split.

"Hurt him?" he growled, slowly shaking his head no. "I'm gonna do so much more than that."

The door behind her flew open, and Livy screamed at the top of her lungs.

"Livy!" her mother hissed. "What the devil are you doing in here?"

She looked back to her father, and saw that he was lying flat again, and appeared to be deep asleep.

"I… I heard Daddy moaning and…"

Her mother entered the room carrying a tray.

"You should have been asleep hours ago," Frances said, setting the tray down on the nightstand beside the bed.

"I was asleep, but Daddy's moaning woke me up!"

"I seriously doubt that," her mother muttered, picking up a bottle from the tray and removing the stopper. "You were probably dreaming. You had a very busy day, young lady, and I suggest…"

"What's that?" Livy asked as her mother poured a thick liquid from the dark bottle into a spoon.

"It's your father's medicine," she said.

Livy could smell it, and it reminded her of the compost pile at the back of the house where they threw their garbage.

"It stinks," she said, wrinkling her nose.

"Never mind that," her mother said, leaning in and placing an arm behind her father's head to lift him. "You get yourself back to bed right now before I decide that little girls up way past their bedtimes wandering the halls should be punished."

Her mother gave a quick look of warning before turning her attention back to her father, forcing the liquid filled spoon between his lips. He sputtered and began to thrash, but her mother held on, making sure that he took every drop, even going as far as to catch the drippings from the corners of his mouth and making sure that those went in his mouth as well.

Father and daughter locked eyes, and Livy knew at that moment that something needed to be done, or her father would soon be gone forever.

"Livy!"

Her mother's stern voice snapped her to attention. "Go to bed—now!"

She quickly left the room to return to her bed, but did not manage to fall back to sleep, the memory of the hopelessness she saw in her daddy's eyes keeping her awake till dawn.

Nira was supposed to be their protector, their shaman. Born with the caul, it was her destiny, as it had been for her grandmother and the others before her.

She was going to be the most powerful the young world had ever seen, keeping the forces of darkness at bay.

Until evil proved itself smarter.

And her arrogance ended the world of the Hiraeth.

The nightmares of the past were as cutting as they always were, sharpened on the whetstone of her memory.

Nira, what have you done?

Constance opened her eyes to the now of a pounding hangover and the knowledge that the memories would be back again to torment her the next time she closed her eyes.

What else was new? You'd think she'd be used to it by now.

Constance lifted her head from where she'd fallen asleep—*passed out was actually more like it*—on a card table in what she liked to call the game room. She'd been doing a puzzle, a 3000 piece double sided monster, the elaborate design she was attempting to recreate made all the more difficult by the fact it was reproduced in black and white.

It was a killer, especially when drunk.

She felt something on her forehead, thinking it might've actually been some brain having squeezed through the cracks in her pounding skull, when she peeled away a puzzle piece. Studying it briefly, she looked down on the incomplete image, and promptly placed the piece where it belonged.

"Look at that," she said, momentarily proud of herself.

Somewhere off in the distance Constance heard an unfamiliar sound.

She listened to be sure, and heard it again.

A knock at the door.

"What the devil," she muttered, getting up from her chair, losing, and regaining her footing after kicking the empty scotch bottle on the floor beside her chair.

Constance strode from the game room out into the winding corridor.

There shouldn't be anybody at her door, she thought, taking a sharp left into a shorter corridor that she didn't recognize, but then again, the house did like to reconfigure itself as well as create new rooms for its own amusement.

There it was again, three short raps of knuckles on the front door.

Normally the house kept potential visitors away, projecting an aura that one didn't really want anything to do with the mysterious Victorian that they had no memory of ever having seen before.

She wondered if there might be something wrong with the home's defenses, and could she potentially be in danger. All food for thought as she finally reached the hallway that led to the foyer.

The ghost of Nana waited by the door.

"Do you know who that is?" Constance asked to a reply of silence. The old woman was obviously still mad at her for potentially shirking her responsibilities.

"I'll see for both of us," Constance said, taking hold of the doorknob, just as the knuckles landed upon the door again.

Knock! Knock! Knock!

"Persistent," Constance muttered beneath her breath, pulling open the door.

"What do you want?" she found herself testily asking, before she even realized who it was waiting on her doorstep.

Livy stepped back away from the door, clutching a purple stuffed animal to her chest.

"It's you," Constance said, surprised at seeing the little girl from yesterday on her doorstep.

"It's me," the little girl said with a nervous smile. "And Chauncy," she said, holding up the purple bear.

"Chauncy?" Constance asked. "Looks more like a Rupert to me."

"Rupert is home keeping an eye on things," Livy said. "Are you gonna help my daddy, Miss Evermore?"

"Constance."

"What?"

"My name, it's Constance. Miss Evermore makes me sound old."

"Oh," Livy said, obviously thinking. "But you are old."

"Thanks for reminding me."

"I'm Livy."

"I remember," Constance said. "Livy and Chauncy. How did you know where I lived?"

The little girl shrugged. "I don't know, I just kinda did."

That was interesting, Constance thought. *Might be something different about this one.*

"Are you gonna help my daddy? He's very sick and getting worse. I don't know how much longer he can fight it."

"He's fighting something?" Constance asked, observing the neighborhood around her. It was a nice day.

"Yes, I think it's a ghost."

"You think?"

"Yes, he spoke to me last night using my daddy's mouth and said that I was gonna die in the house and live there forever."

"That isn't good."

"No, it isn't," Livy said, clutching her purple bear tighter. "That's why I came to see you. Are you gonna help, Miss… Constance?"

"I still haven't decided," she answered with a shrug. "But why don't you come on inside and try to convince me."

Livy hesitated a moment. "You sure?"

"Wouldn't've asked if I wasn't," Constance said, stepping to the side to allow the child to enter.

"How the hell did you get here anyway?" Constance asked, suddenly realizing that she and the bear were alone.

"I took the bus," Livy answered.

"Does your mother know?"

Livy shook her head. "No, I got up early. I didn't sleep good last night after…"

"Yeah, after the ghost gave you a hard time," Constance said, closing the door behind them.

"He was very mean."

"They can be like that," Constance said. "So, welcome to my humble abode."

"Abode means house, right?" Livy asked, looking around as she walked further from the entrance.

"It does," Constance said.

"Who's she?" Livy asked.

Constance was surprised at first, but saw that Nana was still floating in the foyer. "You can see her?" Constance asked.

"Ah huh," Livy said, nodding.

"That's my Nana," Constance answered.

"And the others?"

Constance saw that the ghosts of her people had all come to greet her guest, flowing from within the house out into the entryway.

"Those are people from my life—before," Constance said, growing uncomfortable with the questions. "You can see them too, huh?"

"Yes," Livy answered with a quick nod, her eyes fixed to the multiple apparitions. "They're all ghosts, aren't they?"

Definitely something special about this one.

"They are, yeah," Constance answered. "But they won't hurt you."

"I didn't think they would," Livy said. "They're different from the ghost at my house."

"They can be a little cranky sometimes, but that's about it," Constance told her.

"I can be cranky too sometimes, when I get hungry," Livy said.

"Are you hungry? I'm hungry," Constance said.

"I had a Pop-Tart," Livy said.

"That isn't a breakfast, that's cardboard," Constance told her. "Come with me to the kitchen, and I'll make us both a proper breakfast so we won't be cranky and we'll talk about whether or not I'm going to help you."

"Okay, and Chauncy doesn't need any breakfast," Livy told her as they took a right after the foyer, heading toward the kitchen

"Oh? Why's that? Did he have a Pop-Tart too?"

"No, he isn't a real bear. He's stuffed."

"More for us then," Constance told the little girl. "How do you feel about pancakes?"

It had been quite a long time since she'd made pancakes—cooked anything, actually. They'd come out pretty good, if she did say so herself.

Livy was working on her fourth cake, with heaping portions of butter and maple syrup, as Constance returned to the kitchen table with another cup of coffee.

"You're not gonna have anymore?" Livy asked around a mouthful of pancake.

"No, I'm good," Constance said, pulling out her chair to sit down. "This coffee is all I need at the moment."

"I like coffee," Livy said. "My Mom said that little kids shouldn't have it, but my daddy used to give me sips when she wasn't looking."

"Your dad sounds like a good guy," Constance said.

"He was… *is*." Livy struggled with her words.

"I get it," Constance said, sipping the scalding morning blend. "He isn't so nice when there's a mean ghost rattling around inside of him."

Livy nodded, shoveling another large bite of pancake into her mouth, chewing noisily. "That's why I want you to help so that my daddy will be nice again."

"Who's daddy isn't being nice?" a growling voice asked.

Livy turned in her chair, her eyes growing wide with the sight of the black feathered and furred animal strolling into the kitchen.

"And is that coffee I smell? It's been ages!"

"What is that?" she asked, eyes twinkling at the sight of Kaw.

"Another nuisance that lives here," Constance said, having more of her coffee.

"I… ," the strange animal began, fluttering its wings enough to lift it briefly off the ground. It then dropped back down to the floor on its hind legs, where it bowed dramatically to the child. "… am Kaw! A pleasure to make your acquaintance…"

"I'm Livy!" the child squealed.

"Good morning to you, Livy," Kaw looked over to her next. "Constance."

"Morning," Constance said unamused.

"What is he… what are you?" Livy asked excitedly, wriggling around in her chair.

"I am a nenil," Kaw said.

"A nenil? I've never heard of that!"

"No, I doubt you would have, child, for I am the last of my kind."

"You're the only one?" Livy asked.

"Alas," Kaw said, lowering his pointy face.

"It's all very sad," Constance said, pushing back in her chair and standing. "Do you want coffee?"

"Please," Kaw said, fluttering up from the floor to alight upon the table. "Are those pancakes?"

"Yeah, Constance made them. They're very good," Livy said. She was about to have another bite from her fork when she stopped midway, plucking the spongy, syrup drenched piece of cake from the eating implement's tines and offering it to the animal. "Wanna bite?"

"Why, thank you," Kaw said, gently taking the offered piece of pancake from the child's fingers.

"Really good, right?" Livy asked, smiling.

"Quite," Kaw answered, licking his chops with a long, pink tongue.

Constance returned, placing a mug of coffee down upon the table in front of the animal. Kaw sniffed the contents of the cup, turning his dark brown eyes up to the server. "Do we have any cream?"

Rolling her eyes, Constance went to the old model Frigidaire in the corner of the kitchen, pulled open the door, and removed a small pitcher. "You think this will be enough?" she asked sarcastically, returning to the table.

"I think that should be fine," Kaw said. "Would you be so kind as to…" He motioned to the cup with his pointed, fox face.

"Say when," Constance said, and started to pour.

"Perfect," Kaw announced, as they watched the dark liquid swirl with the added cream, turning a lighter shade of brown.

She set the creamer down on the table as the animal delicately began to lick up the coffee from its cup.

"This is wonderful," Kaw said in between laps. "You never realize how much you've missed it until you have a lovely cup."

There was silence for a moment, except for the sound of lapping.

"Why are you all alone?" Livy then asked, interrupting the quiet. "Where are the other nenils?"

Kaw's licking stopped, and they slowly raised their head from the cup.

"That's a question, my dear Livy, that I have asked myself many times over the long years that I've lived," Kaw said.

"You see, Livy," Constance said, putting her coffee mug down. "A very long time ago I thought I was a really big deal and wasn't paying attention to something that I should have, and the world at the time paid the price for my overconfidence."

"What happened?" Livy asked.

"People died, Livy, Kaw's brothers and sisters all died," she answered matter of factly. "And it was all my fault. That's just something I've had to learn to live with."

"So, that's where all the ghosts in your house come from?" the little girl asked.

"Exactly," Constance said, nodding.

"And, why I'm the only one," Kaw said. "The last of my kind."

"Why aren't there any nenil ghosts?" Livy asked, having a sip of juice while she waited for her answer.

"The spirits of the nenils all moved on when their lives were brought to an end," Kaw said. "They didn't feel the need to hang around. Unlike another species we know, they don't believe in holding grudges."

"And that's a good thing, the house is crowded enough," Constance said.

"Why are you still here then?" Livy asked. "Couldn't you have moved on too with your family?"

"But I survived for a reason," Kaw said, turning his gaze to Constance. "And the nenil didn't believe in grudges, but I on the other hand…"

"It's all a reminder of what I didn't do, and the repercussions because of it," Constance said. "And not to let it happen again."

"That's why you help people, right?" Livy asked.

Constance looked at the little girl, and in her face saw the faces of all she had let down—all who had died because of her—and remembered the vow she had made as she lay upon the surface of a world wiped away by an apocalypse of her own making.

Never again, she swore to the nascent world.

"Yes," she answered the child.

"And that's why you're gonna help my daddy." She smiled then, a smile filled with the relief that at last her nightmare was soon to be over.

"Of course," Constance said. "It's what I do."

"Yaaayyy!" Livy said, before cramming an enormous piece of pancake into her mouth.

"Well, that's settled," Kaw said, having a few more laps of their coffee before leaping from the table, wings spread, gliding to the floor. "I'm glad to see that you've finally come to your senses."

"Don't I always?" Constance asked.

"It's been so long I don't remember," Kaw said, strolling from the kitchen.

"Bye, Kaw! It was nice to meet you!" Livy called after the strange animal.

"Goodbye, Livy," they said, not bothering to turn around. "I'm sure we'll be seeing each other again."

"Okay, bye!" the little girl said. "They're nice."

"Yeah," Constance said. "A real peach."

Livy wiped her face and hands with a napkin and hopped out of her chair.

"Are we going to my house now?" she asked, excitedly.

"Hold your horses," Constance said. "We'll get there, but first I need to gather some things."

"What kind'a things?" Livy asked, following on Constance's heels.

"Well, I can't do the job without my tools."

Constance called it her war room, but it was really a very large, walk-in closet that the house had decided to construct as the years passed by and Constance's battle against evil required her to collect a variety of tools to deal with the multitude of threats that presented themselves.

"Don't touch anything," Constance warned, walking further into the deep space of many shelves, cabinets, and doors.

"These are all your tools?" Livy asked, craning her neck to try and see up onto the highest of shelves.

"Yes, tools of the trade, so to speak."

"Huh," the child said, obviously impressed—*what else would she be?*

"What tools are you gonna need to take care of my daddy?"

"That's a good question," Constance said, standing on tippy toes to check out what was stored there. "Going on what you and your mom talked to me about, I was thinking some simple prayers of banishment might be enough, but that recent business with the ghost speaking through your father's mouth—"

"That was very scary," Livy stressed.

"Yeah, I'm thinking maybe a rite of exorcism might be in order."

"Exorcism, right," the little girl said.

Constance removed a vial of holy water from a metal chest adorned with a crucifix.

"Can't go wrong with holy water blessed by Pope Roland the Vicious, the Forgotten Pope," she said, shaking the vial at the little girl.

"If you say so," Livy answered. "What else?"

She'd taken a small hardback book from a collection of old books on a shelf, her arms starting to become filled with odds and ends.

"Hey, do me a favor," Constance said to Livy, motioning with her chin. "Behind you, on the hook just inside the door, get me my bag."

Livy turned, seeing the satchel hanging there and grabbed for it, immediately pulling her hand away.

"What's wrong?" Constance asked, on the verge of being concerned.

"It's warm," the child said.

"Oh, is that all? It's fine. Grab it, will you, before I drop this stuff."

Livy's hand went for the bag, hovering momentarily before grabbing it again. "What's it made from?" she asked, making a face.

"That's my caul bag," Constance said. "It's made from the caul that was covering my face when I was born."

"It's like skin?" Livy asked, becoming even more repulsed.

"Yeah, kind'a," Constance said. "Babies born with cauls are said to be born with special powers, connecting them to the preternatural."

"Ghost stuff?" asked Livy.

"Yes, that, and other things."

"And you made a bag out of it?" Livy was not impressed.

"Not just any bag," Constance said. "A very special kind of bag, one that helps me do my job."

"Oh," Livy said. "Okay, are you gonna take it?"

"Open it for me," Constance said. "It's cinched closed, but pull it open so I can put this stuff in."

Constance was curious about the outcome of this action, the bag usually refusing to be opened by anybody other than her...

"Like this?" Livy asked, tugging on the leathery opening pulled tightly closed.

It looked as though it wasn't going to budge, Constance's curiosity about the little girl's level of specialness momentarily satisfied, when the bag came suddenly open.

"You opened it," Constance said.

"Yeah, I did," Livy answered. "Could we put that stuff inside so I can put it down? I don't like how it feels!"

"Sure, sure," Constance said, starting to put the items in her arms inside the caul bag.

"There's too many things," the kid said. "They'll never fit!"

"Nah, plenty of room. They'll fit just fine."

The items went in, as did others that Constance pulled down from the shelves.

"How are you doin' that?" the child asked incredulously.

"I told you the bag was special."

"Wow, no kiddin'," Livy said in awe.

"I think that just about does it," Constance said, again surveying the contents of the closet. "If I don't have it, we don't need it."

Livy was still looking into the bag.

"Don't get too close," Constance said. "You might end up inside with all the stuff, as well as some other things that I've locked away."

The little girl quickly pulled her gaze from the opening.

"Give it here," Constance said, reaching out. Livy happily handed the caul bag over to her, wiping her small hands on the legs of her jeans.

"You ready to go?" Constance asked her.

"Yes," Livy said. "Do you have a car?"

"No. I have a house."

"Oh, how we gonna get there then?"

"How did you get here?"

"I took the bus."

"Well, okay then."

Constance couldn't remember the last time she'd ridden on public transportation, but there was something strangely exciting about the experience; the nearly overpowering stench of bus exhaust, the various auras of fellow passengers sitting around her, the view outside the window of a world that she had promised with all her heart to protect from the everpresent forces of evil that threatened to consume it.

It was good for her to get out, to truly see what it was that she was protecting. The changes all had come so incredibly fast; one moment humanity had just come down from the trees and were beginning to walk erect, the next they were riding in diesel-powered internal combustion machines going forty miles an hour down a back road.

If that wasn't progress, she didn't know what was.

Ding!

Constance turned her head to see that Livy was standing, and had pulled a cord hanging above the seat to signal the bus driver.

"Time to get off," she said, moving past Constance to walk down the aisle to the front of the bus. Constance followed.

"Right here?" the driver asked.

"Yes, please," Livy responded as the bus driver banked his vehicle to the right, bringing it closer to the side of the road.

The doors opened with a hydraulic hiss, and Livy thanked the man as she got off, Constance right behind her.

Standing at the side of the road, they waited as the bus pulled away revealing an open area of land in front of them that gently sloped upward and the old farmhouse that sat atop the hill.

"That it?" Constance asked.

"Yes," Livy answered, her tone flat, floating the idea to Constance that the little girl wasn't all that happy to be home.

Crossing the road, Constance and Livy walked the packed dirt and rock driveway up to the farmhouse. There was nothing special to be seen with the old property, a typical structure from the time period of wooden shingles and clapboard. The most that she could see was wrong was that it was in serious need of a paint job, the painted shingles having turned an almost dirty gray, peeling away from the wood beneath, giving it an almost feathered look. But other than that…

"Hold on a second," Constance said, just before the top of the drive. She squatted down by the side of the road, sinking her fingers into the soil.

"What are you doing?" Lily asked her.

"Reading the land," Constance explained. "You can find out quite a bit about a place by listening to its dirt."

Constance listened.

"What's it saying?" Livy asked.

"Not a whole lot," Constance said, craning her head ever so slightly, tuning into the land. There was surprisingly very little to be learned. It was all just dirt, rock, and soil, nothing special at all.

Which, on a property this old, was—*odd*.

Constance stood, wiping her dirty fingers on the front of her pants. "Let's keep going," she said, gesturing to where the house sat.

As they approached the steps leading up to the front porch, the screen door came open with a rusty screech and Livy's mom stepped out.

"I thought I heard something out here," Frances said, her expression angry as she looked at Livy, but brightening upon seeing Constance was with her.

"Miss Evermore," Frances said. "This is a surprise."

"I went to see her to ask if she was gonna help Daddy," Livy explained.

"You went to see her?"

"Yeah, I took the bus," Livy explained.

"I see," Frances said. "And from Miss Evermore's appearance with you here, I'm guessing…

"I'm here to help," Constance said, as she looked around the property, but sensing nothing out of order. From all she could gather, it was just an old farmhouse, sitting on a piece of land with nothing to say. "If we can go inside, we can get started."

"Of course," Frances said, pushing open the outside door, gesturing for them to come in. "Where are my manners?"

Livy went up onto the porch first. "Hope you're not mad," she said as she passed her mother on the way inside.

"Not mad at all," Frances said. "I just wish you'd've let me know what you were planning. I was worried when I couldn't find you this morning."

"I can see how that would be a problem," Constance said, stepping past the woman and through the doorway into what looked to be the kitchen.

"And I hope that she didn't bother you," Frances said, closing the screen and the main door behind her.

"Not a bother at all," Constance answered, checking out her surroundings. "Nice place you have here."

"Thank you," Frances said.

It didn't appear that the place had been touched, retaining much of its mid-19th century charm. Constance still found it strange that she wasn't picking up on anything at all, old homes like this always gave off residual energies just based on how long they'd been around. And this place, having been owned at one time by a mob boss, she imagined that it would have much to say.

But nothing, just like the land upon which it was built.

"We'd talked about renovating, but when the activity began almost immediately after we moved in, we decided that maybe we should wait." Frances had gone to the old stove and picked up a kettle, bringing it to the sink.

"Tea?" she asked.

"Certainly," Constance said, reaching out into the dwelling with her psychic feelers but grasping nothing. "That would be nice, thank you."

Lighting the burner, Frances set the kettle down

and retrieved two cups from a cabinet to the left of the sink.

"And my husband started to get sick not too long after that," she said. She opened a breadbox on the counter, removed some packaged cookies and brought them to the small kitchen table situated in the middle of the room.

"I'm gonna bring Daddy some cookies," Livy said, going to the table and opening the package. She grabbed a napkin and placed four cookies on it. Cookies always make me feel better." Helping herself to one more of the treats, she placed it in her mouth and holding the napkin in front of her, moved toward a stairway to the side of the dining room.

"Don't wake him if he's sleeping," Frances called after her, the kettle just starting to howl. "He had a really bad night."

Constance came to the kitchen table and slid out one of the chairs, sitting down.

"So nobody else?" she asked.

"Pardon?" Frances asked, bringing the two cups to the table, a teabag in each.

"Got sick," Constance said. "Only your husband?"

"Oh, yes," she answered, taking the kettle from the stove and pouring the scalding water over the bag in each of the cups. "It was after we'd started digging in

the cellar that maybe we'd stirred something up and he'd caught a sinus infection or something."

Frances went to the refrigerator and returned with milk, placing it next to the package of cookies.

"Why were you digging in the basement?"

Frances pulled out a chair and sat.

"You'll laugh at me," she said, picking up the string leading out of her cup, dipping the teabag up and down in the hot water to steep.

"Try me," Constance said, pulling the sugar bowl toward her and adding two heaping teaspoons to her cup.

"Not only was this farmhouse gorgeous, and the exact thing that Paul and I were looking for, but…

Constance waited for the woman as she removed the bag from her cup and placed it on a napkin.

"There was also the rumor."

Constance picked up her cup, not bothering to remove the bag.

"Go on," she said in between sips of the hot liquid.

"Paul was a prison guard before we bought this place… before he got sick," Frances said, clutching her tea cup in both hands, staring down into the rust colored beverage.

Constance sat, listening, sipping.

"There was a prisoner there, an old timer that he

got to be kind of friendly with who used to be in Vincent Tomesello's crew."

"The mobster who last owned this place," Constance said, nodding ever so slightly as she collected her information.

"That's right," Frances said. "That guy was sick, dying—lung cancer, I think—but he liked my husband, and my husband liked him. Used to bring him cigarettes, if you can believe it."

"It's a way of shaking one's fist at an inevitable demise," Constance said. "Go on."

"Because they were friends, Paul was there when he passed, but just before he died he told Paul about the money."

"The subject of the rumor?"

"Yes," she said, nodding. She picked up her cup and had some more tea. "I guess Tomesello had money hidden all over the property—didn't trust banks, and seeing that it was all made illegally…"

Pieces of the story all began to fall into place.

"Let me guess," Constance said. "You bought the farmhouse so you could try to find the money."

Frances averted her eyes, totally focusing on the contents of her cup, and smiled shyly. "We really did love the place the moment we saw it."

"And the fact that there might be money hidden

somewhere on the property made it all the more attractive."

"Yes, there's that too." She laughed to herself.

"And that's why your husband was digging in the cellar," Constance said. "He was searching for buried—"

The scream that floated down from the upstairs of the farmhouse was like an icepick to the eardrums and filled with absolute terror.

"Oh, dear." Frances set down her cup with a clatter.

"Livy," Constance said, rising from where she sat, heading for the stairway.

At the bottom of the stairs she felt it, the slightest hint that *something* wasn't quite what it was supposed to be. It was the first time she'd felt anything since arriving at the house, and now her suspicions were totally piqued.

Before ascending, she reached to her side, feeling for the bag made from her birth skin that had designated her protector of her people, and thus the world.

Yeah, we saw how that turned out.

Constance bolted up the stairs, the oppressive feeling of strangeness that filled the air of the stairway growing thicker with her every step. It was as if all the negativity that might've been associated with the house had collected up there on the second floor.

She reached the top, continuing to read the atmosphere before striding down the hallway toward a closed door, emanations of something that did not belong so strong that it nearly drove her back. Taking the doorknob in hand she turned it, throwing the door wide, ready to confront what had been hiding within.

The bedroom stank of sickness and rot, the air so heavy with evil it was palpable.

Her eyes found Livy, cowering in the corner of the room, trembling uncontrollably with fear, as the pajama wearing figure, undoubtedly her father, floated in the air above her.

"It's okay, Livy," Constance said, reaching into the caul bag at her side.

The floating man's body shuddered violently with her announcement as it hung there, his head turning ever so slowly to fix her in his gaze.

"It's about fucking time you got here," he said, his voice sounding as though he throat was clogged with dirt. His body turned gracefully in the air, like a shark gliding through water.

"You've been waiting for me, huh?" Constance asked, her fingers inside her bag, fiddling for the appropriate tool for the moment.

The man laughed. "You might say that, yeah."

He floated there, moving ever so slightly in some invisible breeze. It reminded her of the sway of the king cobra, mesmerizing its prey, as it readied to strike.

"You have me at a disadvantage then," she said, not taking her eyes from the floating man. "Who am I talking to? I know it isn't the girl's father."

"You don't think?" the man asked. "What? You think I couldn't have a pretty kid like that?" He looked quickly at Livy, still wedged fearfully into the corner of the room, before turning back to her.

"You really don't seem like the kid type," Constance answered.

"Ha," the man chuckled wetly. "I hate the fucking brats. Whenever I knew one'a the broads I was fuckin' was knocked up, I made a call to a doctor friend who owed me and that was that."

"There was quite a bit of death around you, wasn't there, Vincent?" Constance asked.

"You got that right," Vincent Tomesello answered. "All'a part of doin' business. People had to die so they would know who was runnin' the show—who the boss was—but then I found out that death had other uses as well, and if used correctly, it made me even more powerful."

The man swooped down from the ceiling, hands talon-like as they reached for her.

Constance withdrew the small, silver mirror from within the caul bag, shoving it into the man's path of descent. The glint coming off the reflective surface cut across his face like a razor and diverted his course away from her, and back up onto the ceiling where he clung like a fly.

"Oh, that was slick, bitch," Vincent spat, wiping at his face where the gleam had touched.

"You like that? It's called a mirror of realization, made by a group of jolly old monks in 12th Century Romania that were forced to deal with a ghost infestation after a plague. It's supposed to show those who look upon it that their time has passed, and they shouldn't be here anymore. Get the hint?"

"I ain't goin' nowhere, lady," Tomesello growled. "And neither are they."

She felt a sudden shift in the atmosphere of the room, and caught a glimpse of multiple shapes as they started to come into the bedroom. There were other ghostly beings now, men, women, and children— babies, adorned in the wounds of their demise.

The ghosts of those who had lost their lives on the farm emerged from ceiling, floor and walls, angrily swarming her, these restless spirits' spectral energies most likely part of the dead mobster's power.

They shrieked and wailed as they swirled about

her, an unrelenting maelstrom of fear, anger, and hopelessness. They tried to enter her, flowing up into her nostrils, wriggling their way past her lips and into her mouth. Constance felt everything they had felt—the joy of living, the sorrows of life's disappointments and loss, the terror as their lives were taken—their spirits locked in place, forbidden to move on to the higher plane.

The weight of their attack drove her to her knees; there was so very much they wanted her to know, to see—even if it killed her.

Constance fought to remain present as she was bombarded by wave after wave of crippling emotion. Far off in the distance she heard Livy crying out her name, and it helped her to focus.

"I should let them have you," the voice of Vincent Tomesello growled in her ear. "But that wasn't part of the deal."

… that wasn't part of the deal.

The last of the mobster's words pricked her back to attention.

"Get the fuck off'a her," Vincent commanded, and she felt the cold weight of the angry spirits fly from her body. "I'll take it from here."

She felt his fingers take hold of her hair, yanking her head violently back so that she was looking up into his pale features.

"This isn't going to end well for you, Vincent," she said, watching as Livy's father's face twisted into something far less than human.

"Thanks for the concern, bitch," the ghost growled, throwing her forward with great force, slamming her into a bureau across the room. Stars exploded before her eyes, and a searing pain that hinted of a cracked rib or two made itself known.

Ignoring the pain, Constance rose to one knee, reaching into the caul bag at her side.

Livy's cries of terror drew her attention, and she shivered at the sight of the tiny girl besieged by ghosts. They were so desperate to share their pain.

Turning her attention back to Tomesello's ghost, she withdrew the tiny, black book bound in the skin of the first demon ever to claw its way up through layers of interdimensional crust, from perdition to an unspoiled world above.

Constance recalled how it had begged and screamed as she peeled the leathery hide from its body.

"What's that you got?" the ghost asked, smacking at her hand as it emerged from her bag.

The blow was powerful, and almost succeeded in knocking the ancient tome from her grasp.

Almost.

There was no need for her to open the book, the

contents in all their many scribbled languages, flowing from within into her fingertips to flood her brain with all it needed.

She began to speak, the first words of an incantation that would bind the restless in place, when Tomesello darted beneath her defenses, striking her again. The blow knocked her viciously to one side.

"Enough out'a you," he said, circling above her.

Something wasn't right, Constance realized; it seemed out of whack, there was no way that a ghost would have such a powerful hold over its host body. It was stronger than it should be.

She looked up in time to see the ghost's descent. This one was going to hurt, and she'd had just about enough pain for today.

The ancient words of binding roared from her mouth as she defiantly climbed to her feet, the guttural sound of a language unspoken for countless millennia bouncing about the confines of the bedroom.

Its momentum unhindered, the child's father, possessed by the spirit of Vincent Tomesello, plowed into her, sending the two of them crashing to the floor.

"Fucking bitch!" the spirit spat, their limbs in a tangle.

She continued the spell, emphasizing each of the

powerful words as she kicked herself away from the possessed's thrashing body.

"GAAAAAAAAHHH!" the ghost screamed, its hijacked body writhing in pain, fighting against the spell that was working to expel it.

"Don't bother to fight it, Vincent," she said, getting to her feet. "You're leaving whether you want to or not."

Constance recited more of the incantation and listened to the pathetic shrieks and cries of the ghost that did not want to depart the man's body.

"You bitch!" Tomesello raged. "You stinkin' no good lousy bitch!"

"Ah, huh," she said. "Sticks and stones, Vincent. Sticks and stones."

The ghostly others had left their torment of Livy to hover around the body that writhed upon the floor, the angry spirit fighting not to be expunged.

"He won't hurt you anymore," she told them, before moving on to the next lines in the spell. There would be other spells, less forceful ones, that she would use later to send the remaining spirits trapped here on their way.

"Livy?" she called out. The child was silent, raising concern. "Livy, can you hear me?"

"Yeah," she finally answered, in a trembling voice.

"That's good," Constance told her. "We're almost done. Hang in there for a little while longer."

"Oh… okay," she said.

Tomesello lay perfectly still, the body he possessed now rendered inert. She was prepared to deal further with the angry spirit, remembering the levels of ferocity it had shown earlier.

She heard the rattling of the doorknob behind her. Glancing briefly over her shoulder, she watched Frances come into the room.

"Miss Evermore," the woman said breathlessly. "I heard the commotion, but the door wouldn't…"

"It's fine now," Constance said, focused on the job at hand. "Livy is over by the bed, but I think—"

The pain was unexpected, her voice temporarily stolen away by the sharp sensation of something penetrating her side, scraping across a rib as it was withdrawn from her flesh.

She glanced down to see the steak knife clutched tightly in the woman's hand, glistening with blood. Frances leaned in close to whisper in her ear.

"I'm so sorry," she said.

Constance stumbled away from the woman and her blade, attempting to comprehend what had just transpired.

"I couldn't allow you to hurt him," she explained. "It wasn't part of the deal."

Again, the mention of a deal, and Constance began to understand that she had been played.

The air shifted behind her, and she spun around to see Tomesello looming above her.

"Sticks and stones," the ghost growled as he raised his arms, fingertips crackling with an energy that made the hair at the back of her neck stand on end.

The ghost unleashed dancing bolts of blackened electricity striking about the room, causing the integrity of the structure to fail. The bedroom floor collapsed in upon itself, crashing down into the first floor below, the sudden and ferocious weight of the collapse causing that floor to buckle as well.

Down into the yawning darkness beneath.

The once untainted air was choked with smoke and the stink of evil.

How did she ever let it get this far? The signs had all been there, but she chose to ignore them, confident in her abilities, believing that nothing could stand against her.

She was the chosen, after all. The shaman—the protector of all that was.

And she had failed.

Nana lay upon the ground that had once nurtured

them, fed them, gave her people purchase, her old body entwined in vines of black that had wormed their way up through the tainted soil to ensnare her in their embrace. The tendrils had held her tight, entering her body through tears made in her elder flesh.

"Go! Leave me," Nana had said, pulling upon the vines that held her tight to the ground, draining away her life. "You must find the heart."

Nira did not listen, a glaring fault that would be her undoing, kneeling down beside her grandmother, attempting to free her.

More vines erupted from the ground, attempting to snare her in their clutches as well, but with an utterance, she tapped into the fire that raged within her, and burnt away the vile tendrils of black.

She tried to do the same for Nana, but the old woman just cried out in pain.

"It is too late for me, granddaughter," Nana cried. "But the world—you must act before…"

The ground shook, convulsing as if in agony, and she heard the screams of her people carried upon the smoke filled air.

"Go!" Nana cried, begging the protector to do as she was supposed to.

The evil had been allowed to grow, hidden beneath layers of normalcy, festering just out of sight.

She should have sensed it, but the evil had become far more cunning. It had watched—*studied*—this protector, had learned of her hubris, and used that regrettable trait to achieve its goals and overpower the world.

Even at the end, Nira believed in herself, that she had the power within herself to thwart what the evil had done—to save her Nana, her people and the land upon which they all lived.

She was wrong—

And the first world died screaming.

The cries of those she had failed drove her from the hold of unconsciousness, back to the reality of the present.

Lying still upon the cold, damp earth of the cellar, Constance carefully tried out her various appendages to be certain nothing had been broken in the fall. Everything worked within reason, and she pushed herself up from the ground, the burning pain in her side reminding her that she had not escaped unscathed.

"Damn it," she hissed, her hand going to where the knife had gone in. It was wet and it throbbed painfully with the beat of her heart.

"You think you're hot stuff," the voice she recognized as Vincent Tomesello said, drifting out from somewhere below. "But that won't be lastin' much longer."

It was dark in the cellar, the air thick with particulates, and she searched for signs of danger. There was something in the air down there besides a shifting miasma of dust and dirt, but it eluded her senses, darting away just as she was to have a better look.

The ground was covered in the ruins from the two floors that had fallen from above, of plaster, dirt and splintered planks of wood. She stepped down onto a place that appeared more stable than it was, her foot sliding and her body following.

"Shit," she hissed, falling back upon her ass, as she rode the pile of rubble down to the dirt floor. The ground beneath her feet was loose, the soil damp, the true floor of the unfinished cellar. As she began to stand her fingers sank deeply into the dirt and she experienced a rush of information.

As the earth began to speak.

It was eager to talk, showing her the passage of time, a history of the land and how it had held a secret for so very, very long.

A secret waiting to be revealed.

A secret waiting for her.

"Constance!"

Livy's voice pulled her from the secret whisperings of the land, and she yanked her fingers from the holes she had pushed in the moist soil. It took her a moment to reestablish her connection to the here and now.

There was something happening here, so much larger than what she had anticipated.

"Livy?" Constance called out, afraid for the little girl. "Are you okay? Where are you?"

Constance stood, searching the darkness still choked with dust.

"I'm okay, I guess," she called out. "I'm in the cellar, I don't like the cellar very much!"

"Stay where you are," Constance told her. "I'm coming to find you."

"Hurry up, I'm scared," the little girl whimpered.

Constance moved in the direction of the child's voice, the darkness doing its damndest to confound her. She reached down to her caul bag, to retrieve a mystical object of illumination, or maybe just a flashlight, to find that the bag wasn't there.

She felt a twinge of panic, eyes darting down to the ground beneath her feet. There was a connection that she normally had with the with the carryall of flesh, but something in the cellar space appeared to be interfering with that bond.

"Don't be afraid, honey," Tomesello's voice

slithered through the darkness. "Daddy's gonna make it all better."

"You're not my daddy!" Livy shrieked defiantly.

You tell him, Livy, Constance thought stalking through the dark, the memory of what the land had teased, making her all the more cautious of the current situation.

She needed to find the little girl, she needed to find her bag.

Constance tensed at the sound of something—of someone's—approach, squinting her eyes as she searched the inky black for the source.

Frances Stafford lurched from the shadows, filthy, banged up and bloody.

"Oh, it's you," she said. "Miss Constance Evermore, the solution to all our problems."

The woman stopped, swaying ever so slightly, sneering at her.

It was then that Constance noticed the knife, the one that had recently been used on her, sticking out from France's stomach.

"You're hurt," Constance said, watching as Frances slowly gazed down to the blade protruding from her body, as if just noticing.

"Vincent… he knew… he knew about you, about the card. Said he would show me… us… where the treasure was… if I brought you here."

"And what, pray tell, would the ghost of a mobster want with the likes of me?" Constance asked.

Frances carefully touched the hilt of the steak knife, wincing. "He didn't really say, and honestly, I didn't care."

"You didn't care that he was attempting to take possession of your husband?"

The woman looked at her, eyes wide in the darkness.

"I really didn't," she said with a slight chuckle. "It was all part of the deal. Paul was nice and all but I realized after not too long that he wasn't going to provide me with what I needed."

"You have a child."

"Yeah," Frances agreed. "That wasn't at all what I needed," she said with a shake of her head. "But this house... I knew it was the answer... that it would give me what was missing..."

Frances's teeth glistened wetly in what little light there was as she smiled.

"... I just had to do what I was told."

"Endanger your husband... your daughter..."

"A small price to pay for what was promised."

"But now you have nothing," Constance reminded her.

"No," Frances said, shaking her head furiously. "No, there's still a chance... the money, it's still here somewhere...

"This is over, Frances," Constance told her. "It ends here and now."

"No!" Frances shrieked, reaching down to take hold of the hilt of the blade and pulling it from her body, like a sword from a scabbard of flesh and blood. "I won't let you take this from me!"

She started to lunge, Constance stepping back from the attack, when a voice cried out.

"Momma, no!"

The words stopped the woman in her tracks. "Livy?"

The child emerged from the darkness, clambering over a piece of wall that had fallen from the rooms above.

"I heard what you said about Daddy… about me and this has to stop!" Frances's child's voice was shaking uncontrollably, a mixture of fear and anger, Constance imagined.

"It's all right, Livy," Frances said. "Everything is going to be okay."

"No it isn't," the little girl said. "This was never about Daddy and me, this was about you… you and this stupid house."

"Stop that, this instant," Frances barked. "You ungrateful little bitch, I should have been poisoning you as well!"

"I'm not listening to you," the child said. "Not anymore."

Constance noticed that the child was holding something.

"Livy," Constance called out, "What do you—?"

It was her bag.

"Livy, be careful with that," Constance said. "Please, hand it to me before…"

The child turned from her mother to hand Constance the bag when—

"How dare you talk to me like that!"

Frances lunged, knife blade glinting in her hand. Constance made a move to intervene but stumbled on a piece of wood, falling to her knees.

"No!" Constance yelled, reaching out, as if beckoning could stop the attack from happening.

Livy held the bag out in front of her to ward off her mother, as Frances bore down upon her.

"I'll teach you to speak to me in that…"

Livy shrieked as the caul bag seemingly came alive, something forcing its way out from the cinched opening, exploding outward in a furious fluttering of black wings.

"You'll do no such thing," croaked a familiar voice, the last of the nenil, Kaw, flying at the child's attacker, driving the now screaming woman back.

"Yeeeeeeeeeearrrhhh! Get away!"

Kaw growled savagely, attaching themself to the woman's face, ebony wings continuing to flap as she flailed.

"Kaw… ," Constance said, attempting to call the animal back, but they would not listen, continuing to attack the woman. Eventually, Frances tripped on some debris, falling backward and striking her head on the wreckage that had collected there with the collapse.

"That's enough, Kaw," Constance told the animal.

"Is it, Constance?" the nenil asked, turning their gaze to where Livy still stood. "Livy?"

"Is she dead?" the child asked.

"No," Kaw said. "Would you like her to be?"

The child looked to Constance.

"I don't think you want that, kid," Constance told her.

"No, you're probably right," Livy sadly answered. "That's enough, Kaw."

"Very well," the animal said, leaving the unconscious woman's body and walking toward them.

"Funny seeing you here," Constance said to the animal, as they sat, cleaning their muzzle with a blood stained talon.

"I thought you might need some help," Kaw said. "And besides, I hadn't been out of the house in ages and decided to hitch a ride."

The animal suddenly stopped, staring off into the darkness.

"Constance, do you feel that?"

"Yes, I've felt something since ending up down here."

Livy came over to join them, handing Constance her caul bag. "Here, I think you might need this."

"Thanks," Constance said, taking the bag from her. "So you can feel it too, Kaw?"

"Oh yes," said the animal, head tossed back, eyes closed as they let the strange atmosphere wash over them. "I... I know this sensation... it..."

A crackling arc of death energy sliced through the darkness, landing in their midst with an explosion like thunder and tossing them away from the point of impact.

"I felt it the minute I stepped into the farmhouse for the first time," Vincent Tomesello, still wearing his Paul Stafford suit, said, floating in the air into a stream of light that trickled down from the hole in the floor above them. "There was power here."

Constance's ears rang from the severity of the necromantic explosion as she struggled to stand. "Livy? Kaw? Are you alright?"

"The place spoke to me like no other," Tomesello continued, hanging above them. "There was something old here... something that had been here for a very

long time, and I knew if I played my cards right I would benefit."

She heard the faint sound of Livy's cough, and knew the kid was alive for now. Constance reached for her bag of skin, ready to put this ghost to rest.

"Not so fast," Tomesello said, another blast of death energy throwing her back. "No more'a your fuckin' tricks," the ghost growled. "Now I get what I was promised."

Constance gasped for air, all the collected pain and sorrow that Tomesello had inflicted in his time flowing through her, and as she lay there she considered his words.

… *what I was promised.*

"Who?" she managed, her voice sounding little more than a frog's croak. She tried, again, this time more forcefully.

"Who… promised you?"

Tomesello drifted down toward her, she could feel the power emanating from him. So much misery… so much death he had been responsible for, and all that pain still belonged to him, a seemingly bottomless well of dark power to tap into.

"The land was hungry when I got here. The house had been empty for quite some time, so I fed it with the blood of anybody who fucked with me, but it was never satisfied, it wanted something more."

The ghost paused, she could feel its cold gaze as it looked out through Paul Stafford's eyes at her.

"I never knew what it was until after I croaked... until after the family moved in."

Tomesello chuckled, a wet rumbling sound from somewhere deep in the throat of Livy's father.

"It was you... for all the hundreds and thousands of years it was here, it had always wanted you."

She sensed it again, rising up from the damp soil at her back. It made her think of another time, another place that no longer existed, but how?

"It spent a good many of those years callin' out, trying to bring you here. Took me and Frances to figure it out."

"Well, I'm here now," Constance said, attempting to rise, but Tomesello again struck her down.

"Yeah, you are," the ghost growled.

"And everybody can get what they want, right, Vincent?" Frances said, crawling across the rubble of her home, excitement of the promise of great wealth heard in her voice. She moved into the light, her face covered in deep bloody scratches and bites.

"Sure, sure, Frannie," the ghost assured her. "But I can't help but wonder..."

Tomesello squatted down beside her, roughly grabbing Constance by the hair, pulling her head toward him.

"What does it get from you?" the ghost asked. "What is it that makes you so goddamn special?"

Constance again sank her fingers into the damp cellar soil, searching for answers to the mystery of this place.

She felt it far stronger this time, a rush of familiarity, a force eager to share its existence. It knew her, and she knew it.

—from the time *before.*

She saw it all—felt it all—in a raging tsunami that engulfed her senses, as if her brain had been torn from her skull and dropped into the churning sea.

She saw the land—Hiraethia—her world as it had been; the verdant lands and oceans lush with abundance, the life that thrived in perfect symbiosis upon it. This was perfection… this was paradise.

And, like the others before her, she was supposed to protect it.

It made her feel some of the pain it had experienced when she'd let it die. The darkness had spread like a cancer, rotting it away from within. The world had tried to warn her, but by the time she'd noticed—

It was too late.

She'd tried to fight the darkness—the evil—but it

had already claimed so much. Hiraethia was dying, transforming, becoming something that shouldn't be allowed to grow.

She had battled against it, but it was all for naught.

The fighting was intense, seeming to go on for a lifetime, but no matter how hard she'd fought, she had known it was too late.

She had to let it go… she had to let it all go.

The searing magical fire unleashed from within her, meeting the ravenous dark in combat—for what, exactly?

She had already lost… the world had already lost.

The darkness and the light came together and for the briefest of moments they were one, existing together in perfect balance.

And then the fire took it all.

Or did it?

L ivy was too afraid to move.

She lay there in the dirt, eyes tightly closed as the residue of death lingered about her tiny body.

"Livy," she heard a voice whisper.

At first she jumped at the sound, thinking that it was one of the many ghosts of the people that had died—been killed—at the farmhouse, but then it called out again and she knew that it was Kaw.

"Livy, it's me," the strange animal said to her. She could feel them closer now, crawling in the dirt and moving alongside her. "And you don't need to be afraid, this is wonderful."

They actually sounded excited, but by what, she wondered?

Livy could still hear the struggle, off in the darkness of the dirt cellar, Constance and the ghost that was inside her daddy. She should've been helping but couldn't; she was so afraid.

"Livy, listen to me," the animal whispered. They came closer to her now, and she could feel the warmth of their breath as they spoke in her ear. "I understand now," Kaw told her reassuringly. "I know why we are here… why Constance is here, why I am here."

She mustered the courage to speak, curious as to what the strange animal was talking about.

"Wh… why?"

"Cause it's all about to change," Kaw whispered, licking the lobe of her ear with their warm tongue.

"It's all going to go back to the way it used to be!"

"**Y**ou gonna tell me?" Tomesello asked, violently shaking her back to the moment, still holding onto the hair at the back of Constance's head.

She could see the ghost behind the man's eyes as he leaned in, sniffing at her body.

"You smell strong," the mobster said. "I'll give you that."

Constance still felt the effects of the death energies as well as the strange emanations creeping up from the soil, as she pathetically tried to free herself from the ghost's clutches. He just held on all the tighter.

"If I was to kill you…" Tomesello suggested.

"Do it, Vincent," Frances said from close by. "Take her strength. The stronger you are, the longer you can stay in that body."

"Yeah," the mobster grunted. "What I'm sensin' from this one… if I was to off her, your husband's body is as good as mine."

"Do it," Frances hissed. "Do it and we'll take the money and leave this shithole together and never look back!"

"Shithole… Ha! I like it. Give me the knife."

There was a rustling in the dirt as Frances looked for her knife. Constance knew she had to break free of Tomesello's clutches or she would soon find herself dead, her death energies added to the gangster's burgeoning powers.

She fumbled at the ground beside her as she searched for her bag, but it was out of reach. Tomesello grunted, shifting his weight toward her. She knew that Florence had given him the knife, and that her time was up.

Fingers digging around her, she found only dirt until—

It was as if the stone had been pushed up from beneath the ground into her hand and, never one to look a gift horse in the mouth, she wrapped her fingers around its solidness and brought it up from the dirt as Tomesello leaned in, knife aimed at her heart.

The stone connected with the side of the possessed man's head with a wet sounding crunch.

She hated to hurt the body the ghost wore, but there was no other way at the moment.

Rolling onto her side, the wound in her flank protested, but she found her bag, and reached inside.

"Vincent!" Frances shrieked, scrambling over the rubble to get to the man. "You bitch, if you've hurt him—"

Constance's hand slid into the bag, finding the item that was needed at the moment.

"Vincent, you all right?" Frances asked. She had reached her husband who knelt upon all fours, trying to help him to stand. "It's all good, we have this—we'll kill her togeth—"

Tomesello brought his hand up, driving the knife blade into Frances's neck.

"Sorry about this, Frannie," the ghost said, pulling the knife along, cutting open the woman's throat in a streaming gash. "But I need your life if I'm gonna survive this, I hope you understand."

Frances Stafford crumpled to the ground, gasping to breathe, clutching at her bleeding throat. Her dwindling life force appeared as a kind of liquid shadow, flowing up from the woman's body, the opposite of the dark blood that now gushed from the wound into the ground beneath her. The death energies streamed up into Tomesello's open mouth, feeding the monster that wore Paul Stafford's skin.

The derringer had been a gift from a Doc Beckham, a diabolist that traveled the Black Hills of South Dakota in the late 1800s, routing out evil wherever his horse drawn wagon filled with talismans and magical elixirs brought him.

She had helped him with a particularly nasty situation involving an awakened nest of bloodthirsty Lamia plaguing the workers of a gold mining encampment.

For her troubles, seeing as Lamia are not so easily vanquished, especially when protected by miners under their thrall, a thankful Doc Bekham had given her the single shot pistol loaded with a bullet that contained flecks of bone from Saint Bethonael of Megiddo, the world's most powerful exorcist, as a way of saying thanks.

The bullet would purge any evil from whatever it inhabited, but would kill the host as well.

Nothing was ever easy.

Constance pointed the derringer and prepared to fire.

Finger twitching upon the trigger, she aimed down the short length of the pistol ready to put a bullet through the eye of the loathsome wraith peering out from behind the mask of the man he wore.

"Constance?"

Livy's voice was filled with question, horror and fear; she could see—*understand*—what was about to happen.

And it caused Constance to hesitate.

It was all the ghost needed.

"Thanks, honey," Tomesello said, darkness streaming from his outstretched fingers, writhing through the air toward her. "Wouldn't want anything bad to happen to your dear old dad, would we?"

Tendrils of stolen death energy punched into her

body, throwing her backward, derringer flying from her hand.

Doc Bekham would be so ashamed.

Like some nightmarish version of a spider, Tomesello scurried across the earthen landscape toward her, carried upon multiple limbs shaped from the darkness.

"You just stay right there, bitch!" the ghost warned. "This has gone on for far too long!"

She went for her bag, but the ghost of Vincent Tomesello had other plans.

It still wielded the blood encrusted knife and bore down upon her.

"I'm gonna savor every drop of your life," the ghost hissed as it leaned in close to where she lay, holding her down as he brought the thirsty blade in close for another drink.

She had put a hand up to ward off the attack when the ground moved beneath her back.

The dirt heaved upward, and something emerged, wrapping itself around Tomesello's looming form and removing it from atop her.

"What the hell is this?!" the ghost raged as he hung, restrained above the cellar.

Constance pushed herself up into a sitting position, marveling at the thick roots that had grown up from the soil to capture the possessed man.

"What's happening?" Livy asked, coming out from hiding, fear in her voice.

"I'm not quite sure," Constance said, motioning for the child to come to her.

Livy ran across the uneven cellar floor, all the while staring at her father held in the grip of the green tendrils.

Tomesello strained against the vines that constrained him. "Let me the fuck go!" he screamed, his voice a roar of ferocity. "What is this? I did what you wanted, didn't I? Let me go!"

"She cannot die," said a voice from somewhere in the shadows. *"She is life."*

Kaw casually sauntered from the darkness, and Constance knew that something was—off.

"Kaw?"

"Something's wrong with them," Livy told her. They're different."

"I can see that," Constance said.

"Do it," the animal said, now sitting looking up at the restrained Tomesello. *"Dispose of the revenant before it can do any more harm."*

"Are you going to tell me who I'm talking with?" Constance asked.

"Do it!" the nenil, no longer Kaw, commanded.

Perhaps sensing that his time was coming to a

close, Tomesello screamed out, vacating the body of Paul Stafford in an attempt to escape.

Constance grabbed hold of her caul bag and pulled at its cinch, opening it wide. She hated to do things this way, preferring to let an earthbound spirit move on its way voluntarily, but not all ghosts were so compliant.

"You're not going anywhere," she said, pointing the mouth of the bag toward the crime boss's spectral form.

She could see his anger, the intense rage of having been forced to leave his host, but that expression quickly turned to surprise, and maybe even some fear, when he felt the tug of the bag.

Constance knew what was inside the bag, all the things she used to perform her function, her penance, but there were also the things that she'd caught—removed—from the world, and locked away inside the mystical sack made from her birth flesh.

The ghost of Vincent Tomesello was about to join them.

"You had your chance to do this peaceably," Constance said. "Now get in the bag."

Tomesello fought against the pull, twisting and turning as he was slowly drawn to the bag's open mouth. She could see that he was screaming, cursing silently as he fought, the vocal cords he'd been using no longer his to control.

"He'll be inside your bag forever?" Livy asked from beside her.

"Yes," Constance told her. "Along with the others."

"Ghosts?"

"Among other things, yes."

"Sounds scary."

"It is," Constance said, remembering all things that had found their way into the caul bag, causing a slight shiver to run up and down her spine.

The ghost fought to the bitter end, spinning himself around and flailing wildly as the hungry bag came closer to claiming its newest prize.

Eager to add to its masses, the bag pulsated with excitement in her hands. Tomesello went in feet first, holding onto the sides. Their eyes locked and he silently begged to be spared this fate as multiple sets of hands from within eagerly gripped his ethereal form, dragging him inside.

The troublesome spirit subdued, Constance cinched the bag closed, and hung it back at her side.

"Is he gone?" Livy asked.

"Not gone. In the bag," Constance answered.

"Can he ever get out?"

"He's going to be... busy in there."

"Good," Livy said. "Can I have my daddy back?"

Kaw still sat, staring up at the body that hung limply in the mass of thick vines. In response to the child's question, the vines unwound their grip upon the man's body, letting it fall to the ground below.

The man moaned softly.

"Daddy!" Livy cried, running to where her father had fallen.

"Are you going to tell me what this is all about?" Constance asked the animal as they calmly watched the child and her father reunite.

"You don't know how long I've waited for you," the voice that didn't belong to Kaw said. The animal turned to look at her. *"When I came to the realization that I wasn't alone, that someone... that you had survived..."*

"Who am I talking with?"

"It is only right that it was you," the animal said, padding closer to where she stood. *"You fought so hard to save us."*

"Who am I speaking to," Constance demanded.

"But the darkness was too great..."

"Who?"

But deep down...

"You had no choice..."

"What?"

... no matter how insane it seemed...

"It was better that we all die than let the darkness spread."

… Constance already knew the answer.

"But somehow I survived… and so did you!"

The ground beneath Constance's feet moved, slowly coming awake.

"It is a sign… a sign that something better awaits."

Blades of grass pushed up through up the dirt, harbingers to the vegetation that followed; the flowers, the vines, the leafy plants, and the saplings that if given time would grow into towering trees and eventually forests.

Jungles.

"A sign that it could all be again."

Yes, Constance knew this voice that spoke to her from within the body of an animal that was the last of their kind, from a time long past, that lived upon a world from a time long before.

She believed she had killed this world, but now…

"Hiraethia can be born anew."

… she knew different.

The before world knew that it was dying. The rot that had infected it had spread, poisoning the soil and filling the roots of all the vegetation that fed upon the rich nutrients with venom.

The evil had been cunning this time, hiding itself amongst the normal ebb and flow of the early world, and by the time it was noticed...

Where was she? Where was the protector? It was the shaman's duty to root out the blight of darkness, to hold it at bay. All who had come before had done this, and the world—and all that lived upon it—had grown and prospered. But now, due to this one, this Nira-Ulah, all was in jeopardy.

The world realized that it was in danger before her, attempting to warn the young woman of the growing threat, but the arrogance of her station blinded her to the signs.

And the darkness continued to grow, and the world to die.

By the time she saw the signs it was already too late, but she tried, fighting back against the encroaching doom with all the magical power that she had amassed from those who came before her.

But the infection ran deep, already having spread, beginning to transform the world into something else.

Realizing what she had wrought, the shaman fought all the harder, perhaps believing that there was something that she could do.

Some sort of miracle that she could perform.

But there were no miracles to be had and the darkness attempted to show her how truly powerless she was to the oncoming onslaught by taking her grandmother and making her watch the Hiraeth elder suffer as she too was corrupted from within like the land around her.

It was then that Nira realized that it was too late, that her sacred duty had been usurped, and that she had failed.

The others that had come before her had faced similar dangers, but all had performed their duties well, quelling the flow of darkness, driving the evil back from whence it came.

But the evil had learned from its failures, observing those that fought against it, learning from their actions until…

They said she was the strongest of them that had ever been born, Nira-Ulah. That on the day she was born, the evils of the world went into hiding.

But that was all part of its plan.

The darkness was cunning, knowing that its absence would help feed the confidence of the world's newest protector, and lead eventually to her downfall.

And it had been right, working its true sway upon the world while its champion remained pitifully unawares.

By the time she realized that she had failed, there was little more that she could do. All the power bestowed upon her by the shaman elders of old was useless to save what had been under her protection.

The darkness was in totality now, inhabiting all that there was; she could do little more than surrender.

But she would not.

The shaman could not bear to see the world that she loved turned to blackness and called upon the power of the ancients, all those who had come before her and fought valiantly against the shadows in protection of this world.

The land knew what the holy woman was doing and accepted it, not wanting to suffer any longer, bearing witness as she wielded the accumulated power of her progenitors.

This was not a surrender, oh no. The shaman fought with all that she had. There was fire, and many cries of the dying as the opposing forces met for what would be the final time.

The land shrieked with each and every strike upon it, wounds cut deeply into the planet's skin, the molten blood spewing from the many gashes, drowning a world verdant with life.

As the darkness fought the light.

At the end, the land was afraid but knew there was

no other way. The darkness could not be allowed to win, to spread its malignance and claim the world as its own.

When it was time, the shaman called forth the power and forged a most terrible weapon, plunging it deep into the beating heart of the dying world.

Bringing about the end of it all.

"*But it wasn't the end,*" the presence inhabiting Kaw said.

"No," Constance agreed. "It was the beginning of something new."

"*Yes,*" the animal said. "*A new world emerged from the ashen remains of the old.*"

"Yes."

"*A new world, but one still tainted by the darkness that you hoped to obliterate.*"

"I guess that's why I'm still around," Constance said, the weight of her purpose feeling suddenly quite heavy.

"*A purpose,*" the voice speaking through Kaw said. "*You have a purpose.*"

The rubble from the two floors that had fallen into the cellar depths heaved upward, falling away to reveal a mound of earth that thrummed with life from a time before.

"As have I."

Kaw walked to the mound, climbing up to sit atop it.

"When the first world died there was a searing pain, and then nothing, but gradually I came to realize that a piece of the old… that I… still lived. At first I was powerless, watching as a new world grew up around me… jungles and forests, life in all its varied forms… civilizations… but I was alone…

Or was I?

I had been close to the end, allowing myself to gradually become absorbed by the new when I sensed you… another from a time before!"

From atop their perch, Kaw glanced to an area of ground that had begun to churn as something slowly began to emerge.

"I could feel you out there, but was unable to communicate. I wanted you to know that you weren't alone that I… that a piece of the past you had been forced to end still lived."

A tree pushed its way up from the soil of another time. It was unlike anything Constance had seen before, watching as it grew in size, mighty limbs with branches like the fingers of skeletons reached up as if to receive a gift from the deep darkness above.

"I needed to bring you here somehow," said the land from before.

"You used the ghost," Constance said.

"I used everything that was available to me. The man craved power in life—and after. His desires would bring you to me."

"He was evil," Constance said.

"He was necessary," answered the land.

"What was so important that you needed to risk the lives of this family?" Constance said, feeling her anger grow, as she looked to Livy holding the head of her father in her lap. "This child?"

"Drastic measures were in order." the land from before said, through the mouth of the animal. *"The fate of the world was at stake, shaman."*

"What threatens this world that I wouldn't be aware of?"

"Not this world, holy woman, but the one before."

Leaves had begun to sprout on the strange tree that had climbed up from the dirt, thick veined leaves that waved in an invisible breeze.

"What endangers you?"

"The evil from the time before has followed you—us, infecting the world's new skin. There is only so long that I can fight it off, to hide myself away, before it pollutes me and the last remnants of a time before—a paradise—dies to memory."

"And you want me to save you from this evil?" Constance asked.

"Yes, save me so that I may live again."

"The old world had its chance," Constance said sadly. "That time has passed."

"No, no, holy woman," Kaw's mouth said, with a slow shake of their head. *"The old land can live again."*

"And how could that possibly be? It's not as if the existing world is going anywhere."

The leaves on the strange tree wriggled vigorously, and Constance noticed a bud, like a clot of blood, had begun to form in the center of at least two of the thick leaves.

"The existing world is rife with infection, as was the old. Perhaps it is again time for a world to end, and a new one to be born?"

"Are you suggesting…?"

"This world will die, and a new better world will grow from its ashes!"

"The existing world is nowhere close to dying."

"You ended one world, you could most assuredly end another."

"I could never—"

"What has this world given you? A constant reminder that you let your people down, that you failed in your designated purpose."

"You're asking me to murder another world!"

"I'm asking you to give the old an opportunity to live

again! This planet was ours first, it never had the chance to show what it could be capable of!"

"You're insane," Constance said. "The multiple millenia spent alone has driven you to madness."

"Oh no, Nira-Ulah, the time has just shown me that this world is but another failure, that despite your struggles with it, the evil grows and manifests by leaps and bounds."

"It's all about patience," Constance said. "I find the evil that survived the end of the first time and vanquish it wherever it manifests."

"This is your mission… your penance."

"It is."

"Then aid me," said the ancient land. *"Help me rid the world completely of evil—be absolved of your past sins. Together we will usher in a new age of prosperity without the taint of darkness."*

A smell wafted up from the throbbing mound, from the grass and flowers and Constance breathed in the familiar scent, remembering a time before when the world was young and so filled with promise.

It was intoxicating.

"Remember," whispered the land through Kaw.

Memories bombarded her with moments of joy and tranquility. It was all so right then, everything as it should have been before…

The recollection of darkness and how it quickly came to claim the land drove the shaman to her knees.

"Constance?" Livy called, watching as she dropped. The little girl left her father, coming towards her. "Are you okay?"

The child's concern was quickly diverted to fear as thick vines reached up from the floor of the cellar, entwining themselves around the little girl's legs, preventing her from reaching her friend.

Livy screamed as she fought against the clinging vegetation.

Constance made a move to go to the child but—

"No, there's no need," the land cooed. *"She doesn't matter, once the old is gone…*

The aroma exuded by the greenery permeated her mind with visions of what could be. She saw this world in ruin, gradually swallowed up by creeping vines and vegetation eager to cover the old so the new could flourish, but before this could occur…

Constance saw herself again calling upon her power—the power of those who had come before—to sterilize the surface, to burn away the infection before the healing could begin.

"Do you see, Nira?" the land whispered, now inside her skull. *"Do you see why this must be done?"*

The land showed her the extent of the disease, the writhing darkness that permeated the replacement world. It was everywhere, riddling the very fabric

of this reality. If anything it showed her how bad it was—how she had again failed.

"I was trying…" Constance said, the weight of her work crushing her down.

"I know you were, Nira-Ulah," the land assured, *"but now it is time to finish that burden, to start again, but this time, with all that we know."*

"Constance, help!" Livy cried.

Constance looked over to see the child as she continued to struggle. The vines had grown tighter, pulling her down against the dirt.

"Don't… don't hurt her," Constance said, feeling a flare of anger begin to grow.

"The quicker you act, the more painless it will be."

"She… *they* don't deserve this," Constance said. "They fight the darkness, in their own way each and every day."

"And once you've done what we're about to do, they will struggle no longer."

She knew the pain of existing to fight that which corrupts. It was exhausting, but she had resigned herself to this task, but what if it could all be over… what if… ?

"Show this world your mercy, and we can start it all again."

Constance gazed up at the tree that had grown

even more in height and thickness, its branches having lowered themselves down, thick with leaves that pulsed with life—with the heartbeat of a world long thought dead. The buds she had seen earlier had grown into full fledged pieces of fruit, hanging heavily within reach.

"Take it," the land commanded. *"From these seeds a new world will grow."*

Shakily, she rose and with tentative hands, reached out, gripping a piece of the ripened fruit. The land sighed as she plucked the offering from the branch, watching as it shifted colors in shades of red as she held it.

"Partake of the fruit and show me that you understand what's at stake," the land said. *"Show me that you agree that sacrifice must again be made if the true world is to live!"*

Constance brought fruit to her mouth, contemplating the offering before taking a bite.

The mound of dirt from the time before pulsed, eager for her actions.

"Do it," the land seductively urged. *"Everything changes with the first bite."*

She sank her teeth into the leathery skin of the strange fruit, thick juices bubbling up from the bite wound, running down her chin.

"Yes," the land praised, Kaw's head now nodding up and down as they urged her on.

She chewed, tasting nothing but bitterness, regret, and jealousy.

"The future is delicious, is it not?"

Wiping her chin with the sleeve of her coat, Constance chewed the last of the bite and tossed what remained of the fruit onto the mound, knowing then what she would do.

A whimper took her attention and she saw Livy, held tightly to the ground.

"Constance, it hurts," the little girl said, squirming against the grip of the vines.

"Hang on, Livy," Constance said, reaching down to the caul bag. "It'll all be over in a moment."

"Yes," agreed the land. *"A merciful end, before a new beginning."*

Pulling it open, she stuck her hand inside, searching for something very specific. She had used it before, the unified might of the shaman—infinite power, yet as precise as a surgeon's scalpel.

The item was deep amongst the many artifacts collected over her plentiful existence, the dark things that inhabited the caul bag fleeing her touch as she searched.

Digging a bit deeper, she wrapped her hand around the hilt, feeling the tingle of amassed power

travel through her hand and experiencing the full effects of the weapon's awakening.

Constance withdrew the sword, crackling with the collected fire of the ancients, blade humming as it came free of the satchel of flesh, and held it out before her.

"I remember the last time the blade was drawn," whispered the land, seemingly in awe of the power in her possession. *"I feared it then for I knew its awful purpose, and how there was no other option."*

She too remembered the fear and the absolute sadness she had experienced as the sword came into her hands. It was a blade of immense power that would be used to wipe away the terrible malignancy, but it was also a weapon of many sorrows for it would be an instrument of ending.

"I accepted my fate, never suspecting my function in a new beginning."

Constance had thought it would be the end for her as well, the world cleansed of evil, along with all life, and she had prepared for the nothingness of eternity.

"The time is now, Nira-Ulah," the land said, leading her to her decision. *"The quicker we stop the suffering, the quicker we can start anew."*

But she had lived, the life energies of a dying world infusing her with everlasting life, and the means to combat the evil that had—like herself—managed to survive.

It was her purpose…

… her penance.

"End it, a new dawn awaits!"

Urged on by the voice of time long past its day, Constance lunged toward the fertile mound, and raised her blade of sorrow…

"What are you doing?" There was fear in the voice of the land.

… and prepared to bring it down.

It must have suspected what she was about to do, reacting with uncanny speed brought on by the will to survive.

"No!"

Vines like millions of boneless fingers reached from beneath the ancient earth, entwining around her legs, slithering up her body, wrapping around her arms, in an attempt to stop her.

But it was too late, for Constance had made up her mind.

The blade of white hot light plunged into the rich soil of the past, and the land cried out.

She watched as Kaw threw back their head, crying out, the scream heard through the cellar as well as within her skull.

Leaning down upon the sword, she pushed the blade deeper.

The ground bucked and writhed, trying with all that it could to throw her from its body. She watched the corpse of Frances Stafford tossed about the cellar floor before it was sucked down beneath the molten earth. But Constance held strong, fighting the resistance from the soil as it struggled to stay alive.

What are you doing? The land cried out.

"What needs to be done," Constance responded, the weight of her sadness added to her actions as the blade sank even deeper.

We were to act together… to bring the old back!

"The old time had its chance," Constance said, fighting back the emotion in her voice. "The new age must be given the opportunity to live."

The land fought all the harder, determined to shake her free, determined to hold on to life as it had for countless eons, but the shaman was stronger.

"Please…" the land begged, its struggle on the wane.

"I'm sorry," Constance whispered, remembering the first time—remembering how she had killed this land before. "I'm so very, very sorry."

The resistance on the sword let go, and the blade sank into the soil as deeply as it could go, piercing the heart of the land.

There was a final cry, the ground beneath her shuddering one last time, a psychic plea for mercy fading from the moment into memory.

She watched as Kaw fell limply to the ground, no longer in the thrall of the ancient land.

The grass beneath her began to wilt, to brown—to die.

"Constance?"

Livy pulled herself free from the now desiccated vines.

"I'm here, Livy," she said, withdrawing the sword blade from the dry, infertile soil.

"What did you do?" the little girl asked.

But she didn't answer, looking at the instrument of a world's demise, as it sparked and hummed in her grasp, the weapon unaware what it had done, other than it had performed the function it was created for. She didn't even know if she truly had the answer.

Opening the caul bag that hung from her side, she carefully slid the blade back into its scabbard of flesh, its home, to await a time when it might be needed again.

"You should have done it," a weakened voice spoke to her.

Constance looked over to see Kaw rising up shakily from the dirt.

"You know I couldn't do that."

"It didn't stop you before."

"It's not like that now, Kaw," she told them.

"Isn't it?" said the last of their kind, turning their back on her with a flutter of black wings and walking away to be swallowed up by the shadows of the cellar.

"Kaw seems mad," a tiny voice beside her said.

"They'll get over it," Constance answered. "Let's go check on your father, see if he's all right."

Livy went to where her father lay. "I think he's gonna be okay," the little girl said.

Constance's eyes drifted in the gloom, landing upon the piece of fruit grown by the tree, whose seeds would have brought about the rebirth of the old.

The oddly shaped harvest lay upon the ground, rotting before her eyes. Constance squatted down, the wound in her side had started to bleed again. She picked up the decaying piece of fruit, shaking the seeds from its core into her hand. They were black with tiny spikes sticking out from their globular shape. Staring at them for a moment, and before she could even question what she was doing, she made the decision and placed them inside her coat pocket.

"He says he wants a drink!" Livy called to her.

That sounded like a really good idea, Constance thought, staring up at the yawning hole to what remained of the two floors that were once above.

Just as soon as they got out of there, they would have a drink.

Constance walked the streets of Clark, Massachusetts, finally on the way for that drink at Derval's before she and the house moved on.

She had wrapped things up just about as cleanly as she could, sending the spirits still trapped at the farmhouse on their way, getting out of the cellar with Livy and her dad. Paul Stafford's condition was better than expected seeing as he'd described to the emergency room doctors that he survived the floors in his house caving in and falling through to the basement. There was no mention of being possessed by an angry mobster ghost. They'd let Livy stay with him at the hospital, setting up a cot for her beside his bed, as he needed to stay at least a night for observation.

When asked about the child's mother, Paul had chimed in that she'd walked out on them a few weeks back, and they hadn't heard from her since.

This seemed to satisfy the woman admitting them, clucking her disapproval as she typed the man's information into the computer.

Getting them both settled into a hospital room, Constance took her leave when an opportunity presented itself, not wanting to hang around for any prolonged goodbyes or intrusive questions.

She'd gone straight home, avoiding any interaction with Nana or any of the other Hiraeth that haunted the house.

There was no sign of Kaw, and she wondered if the animal would ever understand the necessity of what she had done—if they might forgive her someday.

She reached Derval's, grabbing hold of the handle to pull the door open and found it locked.

That's strange, she thought, knowing that the bar opened to the public at noon, but then she noticed the message taped to the door.

Please forgive us, for we are closed today to honor the life of Harry Derval who served his country honorably in World War II, and served a thirsty community in Derval's Pub these last forty years. He will be missed by all who knew him and be spoken of with reverence to those who did not.

Derval's will return to business tomorrow. Thank you for your understanding and your sympathies.

Ian Derval—Proprietor

Constance had suspected when she saw him again that this was probably the end of his journey, and was glad that she had been right back in Hürtgen Forest, that they would see each other again, even if it was only the tiny knot of connective tissue that brought her to this latest task.

That's just how things worked; she never knew the full extent of the people who came and went in her life and the parts they might play.

About to leave, she saw a shadowy shape move within the bar. It came out from the back, stopped as it saw her standing there, and came toward the door.

It was Harry's son, Ian.

He undid the lock and pushed open the door.

"Hello," he said, the sadness of loss in his voice.

"Hello," she responded. "I don't mean to disturb your grief, was just stopping by for a quick drink before—"

"Then come in," he said, pushing the door wider and motioning for her to enter.

"Are you sure?"

Ian nodded, and smiled. "I'm sure Dad would want you to."

They didn't say much as she took a seat at the bar and watched as he retrieved the bottle of Merriman's 12-year-old single malt from its place of honor on the shelf and placed two glasses in front of her.

"This is what he would've wanted us to be drinking," Ian said, removing the stopper from the bottle and dispensing two generous pours.

"I can't argue with that," she said.

Ian placed the stopper back in the bottle, picked up his glass and raised it. "To a better world," the man said, and she raised her own glass in return. "And to the life of Harry Derval," Constance added.

They both drank, savoring the old whiskey.

"To a better world," Constance repeated, the words resonating with her.

"Yeah," Ian said, returning to the bottle and pouring them two more drinks. "It was what my father said before he drank."

The salute echoed inside the caverns of her mind.

"It's a good toast," she said, this time savoring her drink.

"It was all he wanted after what he'd seen during the war—a better world." Ian drank.

"There's still a chance," Constance said.

"A chance?"

"For a better world."

"I certainly hope so," Ian said, before downing the remainder of his second drink. "It's the only one we got."

A brief flash of a world filled with untold beauty flashed before her mind's eye, before it was all consumed in fire.

"Hear, hear!" she said, raising her glass, and finishing the contents in a single gulp.

They had come close to finishing up the bottle when Constance knew it was time to leave. Having said their goodbyes, she promised the drunken man that she would see him again in the not too distant future but doubted that would be the case.

She didn't really see a return to Clark, Massachusetts, but again, with the life she led, one never knew.

The house was still where she'd left it, which was always good, and as she approached it she noticed a small figure sitting on the steps waiting for her.

"Well, look who it is," Constance said.

Livy smiled, standing up from where she sat.

"I was gonna go in, but I thought I'd wait for you out here."

"Pretty early even for you," Constance said, talking to the child from the foot of the stairs. "Everything okay?"

"Yeah, everything is great! Daddy's doing better every day, and…"

The little girl looked around conspiratorially, and came down the steps to get closer to her.

"And we found the treasure," she said, covering her mouth and speaking in a whisper.

"Seriously?" Constance said. "That's great. So it all worked out."

"We're gonna get the house all fixed up so we don't have to live in the motel anymore."

"Terrific," Constance said, climbing the remainder of the steps to the door. "Are you coming in?"

"I promised Daddy that I would help him with his rehab," Livy said.

"Don't want to miss that," Constance said.

"No," Livy said, shaking her head. "He needs me to help him get stronger."

"It's a good thing that he has you."

"Are you leaving now?" Livy then asked.

"Yeah, I really should think about moving on," Constance said, hand resting on the doorknob. "There's still plenty of things I need to address out there."

"Bad things," Livy said.

"Exactly," Constance agreed.

"Oh, okay." Livy started down the stairs, stopping to turn back to her. "Maybe I'll see you again," the child said.

Constance considered the suggestion, and thought that this just might be true.

"Maybe you will."

The child smiled, and with an over the shoulder wave, continued down to the sidewalk, and on her way.

Maybe you will, Constance thought, watching the child until she disappeared around a corner before opening the door and going inside.

The house had moved on, resting someplace between here and there before deciding on where it would eventually be needed.

But until then, Constance had things to do.

Standing in the war room closet, she took the items she had brought with her to the Stafford household from her caul bag, returning them to the shelves where they would wait for her to need them again.

"Straightening up?" asked a familiar voice, just outside the door.

Constance glanced over to see Kaw sitting, watching her from the doorway.

"Yes," she said, placing a very old book back from where she had taken it. "I hadn't had a chance to do it until now."

"A place for everything, and everything in its place," the animal said, casually examining the hooked talon on one of their front legs.

"That's right," Constance said, reaching deep into the bag, and fishing around for anything she might've forgotten. "Are we good?" she asked her friend.

Kaw was silent for a moment, and she looked over to where they still sat. Nana and the ghosts of her people had all joined the last of the nenil outside the war room door.

"We are," Kaw finally answered. "Even though I think what you did was wrong."

"I did what I thought was right for now," Constance said, setting her caul bag down upon a lower shelf.

"For now," Kaw said, "but what if later…?"

Constance did not answer right then, carefully reaching into her pocket and removing the spikey black seeds that she'd placed there from the fruit of the Hiraethia tree.

"We'll need to wait and see," she said, the potential for a new beginning patiently waiting, asleep, in the palm of her hand.

She took a heavy glass container from one of the shelves, removed its cover and dropped the seeds inside.

"But until then,"

She put the cover back, and placed it back on the shelf.

To a better world, she heard Ian Derval's voice echo inside her skull. *It's the only one we got.*

THE END

ACKNOWLEDGMENTS

TOM:

As always, thanks to LeeAnne, my long-suffering wife, for letting me do my 'thang.' And to Harvey allowing me to attend to his needs 24/7. To Mom Sniegoski for bringing me screaming into this world, and to Barry for loaning me your wife. Thanks to the staff at Bad Hand Books for all their amazing support, and to Tom Brown for creating some really pretty pictures that make this book something extra special. To the folks at Halloran Park—Nancy & Bandit, Harrison, Stephanie, Theo and Esme, Dale & Allie, Tom & Seamus, Barbara & Joe. A very special thanks to my Comic Book Homies— Alex & Chris from "Tell the Damn Story," Rich, Craig, Jarrett, Ralph, and Spider-Mans who gave me ham. And an extra special thanks with sprinkles and a cherry on top to Chris 'Clint' Golden for still talking to me.

—TES

JEANNINE:

Lots of love and gratitude to Barry, my saint of a husband for loving me all these years and supporting my ideas, both fully-baked and half-baked. Thanks and love to Julia & Bertie and Randy & Asmani, who never uttered the words "Mom's crazy"—out loud. Thanks also to the convention-attending Achesons, and Matt & Sue and all the Surettes & Beaulieus, big and little, who make me smile. To my HRMS ladies—Cherry, Liz, Mary & Rachel—for keeping in touch and cheering me on. To Alex & Chris of "Tell the Damn Story" fame, and Chris Golden, thank you for accepting me as one of your own. Special thanks to Doug Murano and the family at Bad Hand Books for showing Nira so much love, and to Tom Brown for his amazing, inspiring art. Thanks, LeeAnne, for loaning me your hubby and to Harvey, thanks for nothing. And finally, the biggest thanks to Tom Sniegoski, my partner in crime. You've opened up a whole new universe for me, and I'll be forever grateful.

—JSA

ABOUT THE AUTHORS

TOM SNIEGOSKI is a *New York Times* best-selling author who has written for children, young adults, and adults, and has also worked extensively in the comic book industry, for nearly every major comic publisher, and has scripted such characters as Batman, The Punisher, Buffy the Vampire Slayer, Teen Titans Go!, Vampirella, Pantha, Hellboy, and Young Hellboy. He is the only writer ever to have been invited to work on Jeff Smith's international, award-winning series *Bone*, working with Smith on *Bone: Tall Tales*, and an original *Bone* trilogy, *Quest for the Spark*, as well as *Bone: More Tall Tales*. Tom is the author of the groundbreaking teen series *The Fallen*, which was transformed into a series of movies for television. Some of his other novels include *The Demonists*, *Savage*, and *Grim Death & Bill the Electrocuted Criminal* with Hellboy creator Mike Mignola, which is currently being adapted as a dramatic podcast by the content studio, Echoverse. He is also the author of the popular urban fantasy series featuring angel-turned-private eye Remy Chandler, beginning with *A Kiss Before the Apocalypse*. Tom is currently working with Mike Mignola and his writing partner, Jeannine Acheson, on a new *Grim Death* novella for release in 2025, from Bad Hand Books. He was born and raised in the Boston area, where he still lives with his wife LeeAnne and their French bulldog, Harvey.

JEANNINE ACHESON is new to the world of publishing. A former seventh grade English teacher turned comic book writer and novelist, she wrote her first novel with her writing partner, *New York Times* best-selling author Thomas E. Sniegoski, during the global pandemic and while she was still teaching. Since leaving the classroom, she has expanded her horizons by writing several comics with Tom Sniegoski, including several *Vampirella* titles and a *Pantha* mini-series for Dynamite Entertainment, as well as the creator-owned comic series *Soul Taker* for Mad Cave Studios. Jeannine is currently working with Mike Mignola and Tom Sniegoski on a new *Grim Death* novella for release in 2025, from Bad Hand Books. She resides on the North Shore of Massachusetts with her husband, Barry, and is currently contemplating the secrets of the Universe.

Printed in the United States
by Baker & Taylor Publisher Services